LASSOED

STEELE RANCH - BOOK 5

VANESSA VALE

Lassoed

Cover design: Bridger Media

Cover graphic: Deposit Photos: Sofia_Zhuravets & photocreo

GET A FREE BOOK!

JOIN MY MAILING LIST TO BE THE FIRST TO KNOW OF NEW RELEASES, FREE BOOKS, SPECIAL PRICES AND OTHER AUTHOR GIVEAWAYS.

http://freeromanceread.com

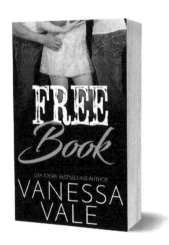

1

ATALIE

"This isn't a date."

"The client isn't here any longer, which means it's no longer a drinks meeting. We're two adults at a restaurant. Alone." My boss, Alan Perkins, leaned across the table and gave me a sly grin to accompany those words.

I did everything in my power not to roll my eyes. It wouldn't have gone over well. He'd been asking me out since my first day on the job eighteen months ago, but I'd put him off. Over and over again. Until now.

Not that this *was* a date.

I watched as the rep from the local chain of retail stores I'd wooed since January walked away—home to his wife and three kids—leaving me alone with Alan.

I exhaled slowly, folded my hands in my lap and squeezed them together. I could be doing so many things at this moment instead of this. Laundry. A cross-training class. Getting a root canal. The meeting with the client had been important, but now? Sitting here in the fancy restaurant with Alan? Misery.

"I don't think HR would consider a client meeting a *date,*" I countered.

Alan was in his early forties. Attractive in that...old boys' club sort of way. He worked out, had all his hair, didn't have bad breath and dressed nicely. He turned heads wherever he went, but not mine. I wasn't blinded by the polish, the money or even the slick smile. I'd heard through the office grapevine he'd been handsy with one of the office cleaning staff, but had kept it under wraps so his wife wouldn't find out. He didn't want to be cut off from her piles of cash, the country club lifestyle or from his job since his father-in-law was the owner of the company.

Being handsy was a nice way of saying he was a cheater. And a sneaky one at that. Or, he wanted to cheat, or thought about cheating. I had to wonder if the employee had enjoyed his advances or repeatedly shut him down as I had. I had to hope she was a smart woman and had asked to be reassigned.

To me, even mentally straying called for divorce. Who wanted to be with a man who even spent time thinking about being with someone else? Fantasy was something else entirely. I thought of Tom Hardy frequently when I pulled out my vibrator, but that wasn't the same as feeling up the people who worked for you.

"...as I said, it's after hours. No work talk."

I blinked, focused on Alan again. *I'd* been straying this time, glancing over his shoulder and catching a glimpse once again of the two men sitting at the bar. Tom Hardy was now bumped down my fantasy list because tall, dark and handsome times two moved to the top. They were sitting down so I couldn't really confirm they were *actually* tall, but they seemed to be. Dressed casually in jeans and button-down shirts, one had his sleeves rolled up, and I couldn't help but notice his corded forearms and big hands.

I loved looking at a guy's hands, wondered all the things he could do with them. Perhaps cupping my breasts, slipping a finger into my mouth so I could suck on it, make it wet so he could brush it over my back entrance, tease me.

Whoa, that was a big, and very naughty, jump.

I squirmed in the booth seat and stilled when Mr. Big Hands' eyes met mine. Dark, intense and full of heat, as if he'd been able to read my dirty thoughts. My heart skipped a beat and I licked my lips, suddenly dry mouthed. His focus caught the attention of his friend and *he* looked at me, too.

Where the first was broody, the second was casual, at ease with the quick smile he tossed my way. Full lips twisted into a wicked grin, his eyes raking over me, settling briefly on my breasts. My nipples pebbled at the thought of that mouth on them, sucking, licking, even giving a slight tug.

I wasn't a virgin. That first time in college had been long ago. I'd learned a lot since then, especially about myself. I was adventurous, confident in my own sexuality, but I'd never considered two men at once before.

Until now. Until these two.

"What do you say, Nat?"

I startled when I felt a meaty paw on my knee beneath the table.

Startled, I moved it away, but the action only parted my legs, which had Alan sliding his own bent leg in between.

My gaze flicked to his and the blue eyes had darkened and the mild CEO was long gone. Instead there was a man who had interest. Desire. Both of which were completely unreciprocated. And he'd called me Nat. No one called me Nat at work. Ever. I doubted he wanted to be called Al.

"Can I get you both some appetizers to start?" the

waitress asked as she approached the table, blocking my retreat.

While his knee was just between mine and not any higher, it was enough to give me the creeps. Trying to get my legs back together was an impossible task; it only made his eyes flare and the waitress think I had ants in my pants.

"Let's get the spinach dip and another round of drinks." Alan lifted up his whiskey on the rocks.

"Oh, no. I don't want anything." I lifted my hand, palm out. "In fact—"

"In fact, bring the spicy wings. I like doing things with my hands." Giving the waitress a broad grin, she nodded, her smile plastered on, then glanced at me. The look she offered screamed *Is this guy for real?* Perhaps she could tell I wasn't interested, and not just in the dip. Or what Alan could do with his hands. As if the idea of him eating wings was remotely attractive.

I sighed again, flicked a gaze at the two at the bar. They were talking to each other—not close as if they were there *together*—but glanced my way once again.

Alan leaned in, which pulled his knee back. Quickly, I shut my legs and slid closer to the edge of the booth.

"We'll talk merchandise," he said, surprising me.

I frowned. "What? You want to talk about the new line?"

Reed and Rose was a small boutique lingerie company. It had been started by Alan's in-laws in the sixties. They'd begun with one shop downtown but had since grown to include three stores locally. I'd been hired as a sales rep to get the items—high-end bras, panties, negligees and other feminine underthings—into chain stores with the business plan to spread regionally and potentially nationally.

I'd had suggestions for a new direction in design, shifting from the staid, trousseau-style items and into a sexier and more sophisticated line, but had been shut down by Alan. Until now. I reached for my briefcase on the seat beside me.

"You want to see the drawings from the art department?" I'd worked for months with them and the other design teams to come up with this new direction. It was a team effort we were all excited about, but hadn't been able to get traction with the higher-ups to make it happen.

His hand landed on mine, stilling my motion. I lifted my eyes to his as I pulled mine out from beneath his, saw over his shoulder that Mr. Big Hands' eyes narrowed at the action.

"This isn't the place to pull those kinds of drawings out. Right?"

I glanced about. The restaurant was high-end, but not ritzy. It was on the first floor of a downtown hotel, convenient for our drinks with the client since it was near his office. The renderings were hand drawn and tasteful, but they were of lingerie.

"Tell me about them instead."

I took a sip of my water, considered his earnest expression. He seemed to really want to hear about what I'd been working on, pushing for, all these months.

"Okay, well..." I went into detail about the line, the bras, the matching panties, the colors and fabrics. When I started on the demographics and marketing research, he cut me off.

"Is this something you would wear?"

I flushed hotly. I loved lingerie. It was my weakness and the reason why I'd taken the job at Reed and Rose in the first place. While I had the degrees and work experience for the position, having a career in an industry I loved was a definite perk. I'd always liked to have pretty, sexy things under my work clothes, but they were for my satisfaction—and possibly the pleasure of a man I allowed to see them—but not for discussion.

Alan's attention shifted to my chest and I knew then he'd only listened to my pseudo-presentation so he could segue to me and what was beneath my professional veneer. I'd dealt with sexism before. Sexual harassment like Alan's that never quite crossed the line. While I'd had conversations with HR about him, his words hadn't been enough to do much to shut him down, especially since the company was owned by his wife's family.

I never wore revealing clothes. I was cautious about it, especially in the industry. Especially with Alan as a boss. My dress was fitted—I was tall and lean with only small curves—but not clingy. While it was sleeveless, it was high necked and fell to my knees.

"Any professional woman would find the line appealing," I countered neutrally.

Alan leaned in further, the scent of his cologne and the whiskey from his breath had me pressing back into the cushioned booth.

"Are you wearing the black mesh number you described?"

I pushed out of the booth, stood, grabbed my clutch. We were *so* not talking about my panties. "Excuse me, I need the ladies' room."

I fled across the restaurant without looking back, leaning against the bathroom sink, staring at myself in the mirror.

Did I want this? A gross boss who was going to constantly chip away at my resolve? Not that I would *ever* sleep with him, but a formal complaint to HR wasn't going to do much. He wasn't going to leave the company. No way. It was his word against mine, every time.

I had to either deal, or quit.

The harsh lighting over the mirror had me wondering why Alan was so interested in me. My hair was a light brown. Mousy. It curled and in the humid air went every which way. I tamed it, pulling it back in a clip, but it always looked as if I'd crawled out of bed. My lipstick was long gone, but I wasn't going to primp for Alan. He'd notice and get the wrong idea.

My makeup was mild, not much could help my eyes which were wide-set and too large for the rest of my face. My mouth too full. Or so I thought. And my figure. I was a small B-cup; not enough cleavage, not even a handful. Wouldn't Alan be more interested in harassing Mary from accounting with her full Ds?

I smoothed down my dress, took a few deep breaths to fortify myself.

Leaving the bathroom, I stopped. Froze, actually.

There, leaning against the wall, were the two hotties from the bar.

"Are you all right?" Mr. Big Hands asked. He eyed me, but not like a lech, but with concern.

"Oh, um. Sure," I replied, giving him a small smile.

"I'm Sam." He angled his head toward his friend. "He's Ashe."

"Hi," Ashe replied.

I nodded, not sharing my name. Just because they were making my nipples hard and my panties damp, didn't mean I wasn't careful. Although nothing about them was sending up red flags on my creep-meter. Quite the opposite, in fact.

"We couldn't help but notice your date and his roving—"

"He's not my date," I countered quickly, cutting him off. "God, no. He's my boss."

Both frowned, narrowed their eyes. Sam was about six foot, dark hair, strong brow, clean-shaven square jaw. His white dress shirt showed off his broad shoulders and well-muscled physique. Ashe was a few inches taller, leaner. A Matthew McConaughey lookalike with lighter brown hair, cut longer with a wave to it. Defined cheekbones and close-cropped beard. The two of them ticked off every one of my 'what made me hot' boxes. It was instant, intense and made my mind wander to dark and slightly naughty places.

While we weren't the only people in the hallway— a few other patrons moved past us to the restrooms and the din from the main seating area was a reminder we weren't far from others—I felt as if we were all alone. Their focus was on me, only me.

"Boss? And he touches you like that?" Ashe asked. "Unless you want it, but based on your reactions, it doesn't seem like you do."

"Him?" I laughed. "No, I don't want him."

I want you. Both of you with whipped cream and a cherry on top. Maybe just the whipped cream.

"Then leave," Ashe added.

"I'd love to duck out, but he *is* my boss and I'll have to see him at the office tomorrow. And, my briefcase is back at the table," I added the last, suddenly remembering. Crap.

"Sounds like it's time to buy a new briefcase," Sam said.

I smiled, then laughed. They smiled, too, as if we'd shared a small secret. "Maybe. I'll make my excuses, although I would like him to consider my product line we'd talked about."

When they both watched me with interested expressions, I waved my hand through the air, shrugging off my comments. These two didn't need to hear about my work. "I'm used to it. To him. It's nothing."

"It's not nothing. *You're* not nothing."

My mouth fell open at the vehemence in Ashe's tone, the way Sam shook his head in agreement. "Oh, um, well, that's sweet."

It really was.

"We're not always sweet." Sam's words were like a promise, a dark one, and I shifted on my heels, rubbing my thighs together. I could only imagine how not-sweet he could be. Whispering dirty words in my ear as he held my hips and fucked me from behind? Tangling his fingers in my hair as he held my face still so he could fuck my mouth? Grip my ankles as he held them at his shoulders as he slid in and out of my pussy with his big cock?

Oh yeah, I had no doubt they could be *not-sweet.*

"We can beat him up for you."

Now I did laugh at the thought of the two of them dragging Alan out behind the restaurant's dumpster, although they weren't smiling. I stifled the sound. "You're serious."

Chivalrous and sexy.

Ashe put his hands on his hips, angled his head out toward the main part of the restaurant. "I assume you're used to Mr. Grabby Hands. That this isn't your first rodeo."

I rolled my eyes. "No, not my first rodeo and I'm used to him. HR can't do much and now that the client's left, this is now a dinner to him. A *date.*" My fingers made the little quote motion.

"You just let us know, sweetheart, and we can take care of him."

They didn't know me but were willing to beat up my lecherous boss. *Sweet.*

"That's the um, well, nicest thing I've heard in a while."

It was. I'd been on a dateless streak for so long that I'd forgotten what a nice guy was like. A nice guy or *two.* They were open and honest, sincere and prepared to drag Alan and his chicken wings outside and teach him a thing or two. I hadn't had anyone stand up for me in a long time.

And I hadn't been so attracted, so turned on by a man—two men—in...ever. Instant heat, attraction. God, the chemistry was off the charts and we'd barely exchanged names. And I'd rather have them *take care* of me instead of Alan.

"We can rescue you, if you want," Ashe said. I noticed his eyes weren't that dark after all, more of a bottle green.

"Really?"

"Sure. Just give us a sign and we'll get you out of there," he added, tugging on his ear like a third base coach in baseball.

I smiled at the motion and copied it, careful so I didn't yank off my earring. "Do this and you'll save me?"

"That douche canoe can paddle his own fucking boat."

I couldn't help but laugh at Ashe's words. Again. I loved the way he was mad for me, that he wasn't remotely like Alan. "It's his wife's job to take care of that boat, not me."

"Married? God, he's even worse than I thought," Sam grumbled. "Sweetheart, you don't seem like the kind of woman who really needs saving. I bet you can take care of yourself, but why should you have to? Why should you be stuck with that asshole just because he's your boss? It's after hours. Your time. You've got two big guys to help you out."

Help you out. Yeah, I could think of several ways they could help me out. Their hands on my body, discovering I was wet for both of them. I had no doubt they could make me forget all about Alan with some incredible orgasms. Crazy thoughts. I'd just met these two and I was thinking about sex with them. But the connection, I couldn't understand it, but I was drawn to them like a magnet.

I looked down at the wood floor, ran my hands over my thighs. When had my palms gotten so damp? And speaking of damp...my panties were dainty silk and couldn't handle these two. I took a deep breath. God, they even smelled good. Soap or woods or something manly. Or, perhaps, just man.

"Thanks. I'd, um...better get out there." I thumbed over my shoulder. I didn't want to go. I wanted to stand here and bask under their honest perusal, open interest and well, kindness. Oh, and just keep taking in their gorgeousness. I wanted to see what else they had to say, to learn more about them than just their names. I wanted to run my hands over their hard bodies, learn what made their breaths catch, what made the bulges in their jeans even more impressive.

Ashe tugged on his ear again, as if to remind me of the signal. As if I'd forget it, or the way his wavy hair brushed his fingers. I wondered if it was as silky soft as it looked. And then there was the smile, the slight turn of his lips, the playfulness. But seriousness as well. One ear tug and I knew he'd—they'd—be there to help me out.

"Nice to meet you…"

"Natalie," I finished Ashe's sentence, remembering I hadn't shared my name, smiled. "Nice to meet both of you, too."

"Natalie," Sam repeated, as if testing my name on his tongue. I loved the deep timbre of his voice, and wondered if it would sound the same when he called it while filling me with his cock.

I swallowed, then smiled. Hopefully, the hallway was dark enough to hide the way I flushed at just his tone.

I gave them both one last glance, checking out every nuance. Not only were they so darn hot, but they were *nice,* too. Sweet, even, but I didn't dare call them that. And then their scent followed me. Spicy, woodsy. Male. Breathing them in made me hot and dizzy and aroused. It was as if pheromones just poured off them and I sucked them up as if I'd been in a drought. Which I had, a sex drought.

There wasn't any more reason to linger, and Alan would certainly start to wonder if I'd fallen in or something, so I made my way back to the table. I took in the new glass of whiskey and appetizers in front of him. He was shoveling some dip onto a wedge of pita bread as I sat back down.

"I ordered for you."

I watched him take a big bite, chewed. A bit of spinach clung to his lip. He grabbed his whiskey, washed it down.

"I'm not staying." I hooked my hand into the strap of my briefcase.

"The night's young. So are you."

I crinkled up my nose in disgust. Looking over his shoulder, I saw Ashe and Sam back at the bar. They'd lost their stools when we were in the hallway, but they leaned against the wood surface where I could still see them. Ashe was talking with the bartender as Sam glanced my way. Why was I still sitting with this loser when I could be with them?

"I have an early morning workout class." I stood once again, sliding my briefcase across the booth. His hand settled on my thigh as I faced him.

"Just as I thought. Nice and toned."

Aaaaannnnnnd we were done.

I was perfectly safe in the restaurant. I could whack Alan in the head with my briefcase. While the laptop might not survive, it would be worth the sacrifice to ring his dumb-ass bell. I could scream and it wasn't like I was in a dark alley. A restaurant full of people was safe. I could even just walk away. But I didn't want to do any of that. I wanted Ashe and Sam, so I lifted my right hand to my ear, gave it a little tug.

While I'd just met the men, and in the restroom hallway of a restaurant nonetheless, I knew they'd come to me. They'd rescue me. They'd take care of me.

I *knew*. How? I had no idea. I just knew they would. And it felt really damn good.

2

AM

"WE'RE IN TROUBLE," Ashe said to me, offering a nod of thanks to the bartender as he delivered our beers.

The downtown restaurant was busy, filled with the lingering Happy Hour crowd and those having dinner. With lots of dark wood, modern lighting and subtle music, it had a strong urban vibe. Nothing like Montana where *urban* wasn't cool. Urban was right here in the middle of Boston, over two thousand miles away. Being a native of the Big Sky state, I hated crowds, tall buildings, the fast pace. But, the bar had good beer and the view was great. Especially of one specific brunette with long legs and a wicked smile.

"Totally fucked." I took a sip of the cold brew, glanced at the woman we'd spent three weeks trying to find. There had been a few pictures of her online, but not many, and none that did her justice. Especially not up close.

Holy shit, she was gorgeous. Smart, too, based on the way she'd had two men hanging on her every word. One had *actually* been listening, having a true back and forth conversation with her. The other had been faking it, nodding and drinking his whiskey, letting her do all the work.

Yes, work. It was clear to me, to anyone in the restaurant, it had been a business meeting. Not only was she dressed in smart business-wear, she'd passed over some papers she'd pulled from a briefcase to the men sitting across from her, used a pen to point to them as she spoke. From the client's body language, he'd been pleased with whatever she'd been pitching.

The forty-five minutes they'd met had given us the opportunity to study her openly, so focused she was on her job that she hadn't noticed us. Thankfully, because it had taken me probably five minutes to haul my tongue back in my mouth and another few to realize I'd been outright ogling. Like a fucking teenager and his first magazine centerfold. I knew her general details inside and out, but not her measurements, although by looking at her, I guessed 34-24-34.

Natalie Bartlett. Twenty-seven. Single. Johns Hopkins undergrad, Penn for her MBA. Apartment owner. Drove a Subaru. As an account executive, she probably earned a decent salary, but didn't flaunt it. She didn't flaunt herself either. Her dress was a dark navy. While her arms were bare, the cut was modest. Somehow, conservative looked sexy on her, especially with the killer heels.

"Has your dick ever gotten hard because of a client?" Ashe asked, leaning in. As investigators, we were hired to find people. Perhaps a man-on-the-side or a mistress. In this case, a long-lost daughter. Or, as we'd just discovered, the one we'd been waiting for.

I shifted on the stool because he was right, my dick was hard. If I got up, I'd be arrested if I didn't get myself under control. "Fuck, no. At least not until now. What is it about her?"

Ashe laughed. "Those tight little curves? Those sharp eyes? How about the full lips?"

When she'd stood to shake hands with the client before he left, we'd gotten the full effect. Tall and lithe, she had a runner's physique. Toned muscles, narrow hips, small, pert breasts. And those heels. Yeah, I had a thing for a woman in stilts. I wouldn't even have to lean down much at all to kiss her. But I'd drop to my knees, part her thighs and discover her sweet scent if she just breathed the word *yes*.

And to top that hot body off was, literally, that

wicked-smart brain of hers, and that combination was sexy as hell.

I turned back to Ashe. "I don't care if she's the client. I want her."

He studied the condensation on his glass, then glanced at Natalie. She'd looked our way a few times since she'd returned from our little chat by the bathrooms, her cheeks pinking each time, her eyes flared with obvious interest. But that was totally wasted because instead of being with us, she was alone with her boss who was plowing through some spinach dip as if he hadn't eaten all day.

"Riley, of all people, will understand," he replied, taking a sip of his beer, putting it back on the coaster.

As lawyer for the Steele estate and the guy who'd hired us to track down Natalie Bartlett, he'd taken one look at Kady Parks—the first of the five heiresses to arrive in Barlow—and decided she was his...and Cord Connolly's. It had been love—and lust—at first sight for them and there was no fucking way either of them would be pissed if we felt the same way for Natalie Bartlett.

I laughed at that. "Yeah, right? How long did he wait before he made a move on Kady?"

"The way I heard it, they knew she was theirs in the airport baggage area, but waited about four hours to claim her."

"And knock her up."

I grinned, thinking of the baby girl they—Kady, Riley and Cord—now had. Cecily, named after Kady's late mother. Born in February with a mop of red hair just like Kady, she had both her fathers wrapped around her tiny fingers. And it was only going to get worse. That girl wasn't going to be able to date until she was thirty, and they'd be cleaning their guns when the guy picked her up.

As for the other three Steele sisters who'd arrived in Barlow, it had been the same way for them. Instalove for Cricket and her three men. Penny had wrangled her two husbands from the get-go. Even Sarah—who had surprised all of us as being one of Aiden Steele's daughters because she was from Barlow—had married quickly. She'd known about her dad and kept it secret, at least until the past winter.

And it had been our job to track down the fifth and final Steele heiress. Natalie. She might be single, but that was about to change. Her social media was switching to *In A Relationship* the second we got her alone. She just didn't know it yet.

"Did you catch her scent?"

"Lemons," I replied. We'd gotten close enough to her in the back hallway to pick it up. To see the dark color of her eyes, her full lips. Every inch—*clothed* inch —of her up close. I was eager to see the rest of her as soon as fucking possible. I'd never wanted a woman so much in my life. One look and... bam. Hit by a fucking two by four. I was ruined for all other women.

And I'd been right. With her heels, she was only a few inches shorter than me. I wouldn't have to bend in half when we fucked. "Yet we're over here while that douche is putting his moves on her."

"It's her boss. She's handled herself well so far." Ashe didn't seem any happier about it than I was, but was proud of her to be smart and strong enough to deal with stupid shit like inappropriate advances herself.

"She doesn't have to," I countered. "The handsy bastard needs to have a talking to. I can see his wedding ring from here," I grumbled, watching the expression on Natalie's face change to disgust.

She stood and he put his hand on her thigh. Her fucking thigh. Yeah, the asshole was walking out of here with a stump.

With her free hand, she tugged on her ear as she gave him the evil eye.

We were at her side in seconds, but in that time, she'd grabbed his palm, turned it clockwise so it faced the ceiling. It wrenched his shoulder and he leaned in, trying to relieve the pain I could see on his face.

"Natalie?" I asked, interrupting our girl at work. My dick got hard just watching her take care of herself.

She stepped back, letting dickwad's hand fall away. He glanced up at us, as he rolled his shoulder and opened and closed his fingers. Even after being so blatantly reprimanded, a grin spread on his greasy mouth as he looked up at us. He wasn't contrite in the slightest, he just gave me a look of a kid caught with his hand in the cookie jar.

Those cookies aren't for you, fucker.

"Yes, oh hi! Sam, wow, it's been a long time," Natalie said, a tad breathlessly. I knew it was because she was flustered and—hopefully—angry at her boss for being such a prick. Also, being forced to do something about it. Putting him in a wrist lock probably hadn't been what she'd wanted to do in a restaurant. Her cheeks were pink. "Ashe, too."

"You look great," he added, leaning in and giving her a kiss on her cheek.

Smart guy. I wish I'd thought of that. Then I'd know how soft her skin was.

"The last time we got together, we had to cut it short," I continued. "It's too bad you couldn't *come* with us then. You can now, if you want."

Yeah, we could totally make her come.

She blushed at the secondary meaning of my words, then grinned. Yeah, she was fucking smart. I loved that brain of hers. She knew exactly what I meant, what I was offering her. It was bold, forward even, but the connection was real. I didn't want to scare her off, but I definitely wanted her to know what we wanted. *Her.*

Natalie cleared her throat, eyes on me. It was as if the boss and everyone else in the restaurant just disappeared. "You're right. I would really like to come with you." She looked to Ashe and her gaze was full of feminine appreciation. "Both of you."

She afforded her boss a brief, annoyed glance. "I'm done here."

"Great," I said, holding my hand out to take her briefcase.

"Nat, aren't you going to introduce me to your friends?" Boss man asked, a piece of spinach flying out of his mouth and landing on the floor.

Wrinkling her nose, she gave him a narrowed passing glance. "No." Instead of handing me her bag, she put her free hand in mine. *Fuck yes.* "Goodnight, Alan. Tell your *wife* I said hello."

Ashe stepped back to let her lead the way. I gave her hand a little squeeze and we headed out of the restaurant. Out of the corner of my eye, I saw Ashe leaning down, speaking to the bastard, hopefully threatening him with the need for a prosthetic if he touched her again, but he quickly caught up to us.

Once out on the sidewalk, but away from the entrance, she stopped, turned to face both of us. The front of the restaurant was well lit, the street busy. It was just getting dark, the air chilly.

"Thanks for your help."

She hadn't tugged her hand from mine and I had no intention of letting go until she did so.

"From what we saw, you didn't need any help from us," I said, letting her know we'd been impressed.

Even though she'd put Mr. Hands in his place, Ashe was still pissed, but trying to hide it from her. She had enough problems with her boss without taking on his feelings about it. "I didn't want you to leave that hallway without us, to go back to that fuckwad," he said. There was a sharp bite to the tone, but by looking at him, it was because he was aroused, not upset. "I didn't get a chance to..." He wiped the back of his hand over his mouth, eyed Natalie. Yeah, he'd found her ninja routine hot as hell, too.

"To what?" she asked, her voice low, husky.

He closed the distance between them, put a hand on her hip and walked her backward so she was pressed against the brick wall, one hand planted above her head. They were in shadow and had a hint of privacy. A little moan escaped her lips right before he kissed her.

I tucked my hands in my pockets and watched the street, although I kept one eye on Natalie. She looked fucking gorgeous, her hands curling into Ashe's shirt at his waist, her head tilted back against the wall. I had no jealousy toward my friend. I would share this woman, but with only him.

He lifted his head and she smiled, then bit her bottom lip. "Wow."

"Sweetheart, I can get you to say more than wow."

She arched a brow in response.

I approached and Ashe moved out of the way. "My turn."

"Your—"

I didn't cut her off with my mouth, but I pulled her into me, looked down into her eyes. Eyes that were blurred with arousal that Ashe had stoked. "My turn," I repeated. "Say you want both of us, sweetheart. And if I kiss you, you're not going to knee me in the balls or break my fingers."

Surprise widened her eyes slightly, but it was followed by a small grin. I didn't see a hint of panic at my words. No, she wanted both of us. She'd been thinking about it ever since we caught her gaze that first time across the restaurant. She just hadn't realized we'd felt the same way.

"No ball busting."

I cupped her jaw with my palm, the other hand at her hip. If I slid it two inches lower, I'd be cupping that tight ass. But not yet, I had to hear the one word that kept all this going.

"Yes," she breathed and I almost came in my pants.

I smiled, then lowered my head, watched as her eyes fell closed just before my lips met hers.

Sweet, soft, tentative, then all of a sudden bold. Her

tongue met mine and her hand went to the back of my neck, tangled in my hair and held me in place.

Fuck, she tasted to so good. Perfect.

"I don't want to let you go," I said, our lips a breath apart. "You feel too perfect in my arms. You taste too good." While she wasn't pressed up against the wall as she'd been when Ashe had kissed her—she had to have felt how hard he was—there was no doubt she couldn't miss the press of my dick against her belly. That I wanted her. "But I don't want to keep doing this here."

Her dark eyes held mine, and when Ashe stepped close, she looked to him. "This is crazy, but I don't want you to let me go."

Fuck, yes. The words I wanted to hear, the consent we needed. Ashe took her hand, lifted it to his mouth and kissed her knuckles.

"We're staying at the hotel," I said, angling my head back toward the restaurant. Just past it was the entrance to the hotel lobby. "Come to our suite and we can continue kissing you."

It was obvious what we wanted, but kissing a guy on a busy street was a lot different than going to his hotel room.

"I know you don't know us, but you're safe with us. We would *never* hurt you." I brushed her hair back from her face, felt the silky strands tangle in my fingers.

"Will you come with us?" Ashe asked again.

She looked between us, bit her lip. "I might want..."

"What?" Ashe asked, taking a step closer. "What do you want?"

I watched as her chest rose and fell with each little pant. Her nipples were defined beneath her dress and I felt a shiver beneath my palms. "More than kissing."

3

ATALIE

THIS TIME, Ashe took my hand. Big and warm, I felt callouses on the palm. The hold was gentle, but I knew he could be demanding. That kiss against the wall outside the restaurant...I'd be using that memory the next time I pulled my vibrator out of my drawer. Holy hell, it had been scorching. A little bit dominant, a whole lot possessive. It had been as if he couldn't help himself, that he'd been waiting to kiss me and his very thin, weak thread of control had snapped.

I liked that idea, of me destroying his control. I couldn't wait to see what happened next.

And not just with the tall, sexy Ashe, but Sam, too.

Solid and tempting, his kiss was so different than his friend's. Equally eager, he sank into the kiss, into the feel of me being in his arms. He licked into me, exploring, learning, his hands holding me close as if a kiss to Sam was a full body experience.

I'd been with men before, but nothing like these two. I felt...safe. And while I hadn't been thinking about my safety when their tongues were in my mouth, subconsciously I knew I was okay, that being with them was a good thing. I may have just picked up two men in a bar, but it was *more*.

I sensed it, felt it with every fiber of my being. The chemistry, the connection, it was deep. Meaningful. I'd had a girlfriend who'd told me she'd known on a first date with a guy that she was going to marry him. A stranger to her, and yet, she was positive. And it had been true. Five years and two kids later, they were still rock solid.

I wasn't considering marriage with Ashe and Sam —insane! But I knew that as they led me across the lobby and into the first available—empty—elevator, this was what I should do. I needed to do it, to be with them. When Ashe turned to me and pressed me back against the wall, I sighed. Reveled in the feel of him. I felt every hard inch of him, some places *extra* hard. And thick. And long. God, his cock was big. Really big.

A twinge of...something made me take pause. My mind had been full of thoughts of them, but what did they think of me? Did they think me a slut to go with them? "I...I don't do this," I admitted.

"Ride in an elevator?" Ashe asked.

My head was tilted back to meet his eyes and I saw humor there. His green gaze darkened and, this close, I could see flecks of whiskey-colored brown.

"No, pick up a man. Well, I've never picked up two before," I admitted.

He slid a fingertip down my cheek, along my neck, his gaze following the motion.

"And, I've never gone with someone to a hotel room before," I added, making it clear they knew this was a first.

The doors slid open and Ashe stepped back. Sam led the way, opened the door to their suite and in seconds, I was within, the door clicking shut behind him.

A flick of a switch and a lamp came on. Soft lighting filled the room. The view from the wall-to-wall windows was impressive. The entire city laid out before us from this floor. I walked over to it, stared. The view was pitch black with dots of colored lights everywhere. Looking down, way down, cars moved along the street, people walked on the sidewalk. It was quiet here. Like a retreat from the world.

I felt one of them approach, but he didn't touch. "Get your phone out, Natalie. Text a friend. Let her know where you are."

I turned about, faced Sam. I hadn't even thought of that, of my safety more than the gut feeling that these two weren't dangerous. They might break my heart, but they wouldn't hurt me. His words proved they were thinking of me, of what was best. I pulled my phone from my clutch, then texted my friend, the one who'd probably understand why I was sending her a note with the name of the hotel and the room number, that she wouldn't judge me for doing something so...crazy. Good crazy, not bungee jump-off-a-bridge crazy. As my fingers flew over the screen, Sam shared his full name as well as Ashe's, which I added to my text.

After I hit send, I looked up at him, nodded.

"Good girl." He reached out and took the cell from me, my clutch as well, and set them on the TV table. "We're glad you're here, but you need to feel safe, that we're not going to do anything to you—with you—that you don't want."

"That's right, sweetheart," Ashe added, settling his hands on his narrow hips. There was something about a guy in a dress shirt. The buttons, the open collar. The casualness of it with jeans. Perhaps it was thinking earlier they had on suits and had dressed down. With the sleeves rolled up, it was as if they now had all the time in the world for, well...me. "We can just talk. Order room service. Get to know each other."

I glanced around, took in the space. Sam stepped back to allow me to wander, take it all in. It wasn't a typical hotel room. Out on the street, Sam had said it was a suite. We were in a living room area, a couch facing a large, flat screen TV on a wall, two comfortable chairs on either side. A large tufted ottoman was used as a coffee table. There was also a small dining table and chairs, kitchenette. On each side of the room, there was a door which I assumed went to a bedroom, one for each of them. I didn't even know what they did to afford such a room.

"You're from out of town," I said over my shoulder, stating the obvious and changing the topic of conversation. Although, they could have been locals who got a hotel room and picked up women at the bar for a night of fun. They didn't have a trace of a Boston accent, but that didn't mean much any longer.

"That's right. Montana," Ashe said. "In town for work. We can talk about it if you want, or—"

I spun about, faced them. They hadn't moved, Ashe's hands still on his hips. They were *so* male. The need I had for them was almost visceral, as if my cells recognized theirs. Neanderthal genes? Caveman? Had they just dragged me back to their cave, but the modern-times version? Did I want this? Them?

If I said I wanted to leave, I knew they'd hold the door open for me, even call the elevator to their floor. We could sit on the couch and talk. But we could have done that at the bar. I didn't want a getting-to-know-you window. Because while I *didn't* know anything about them, I knew *of* them. Of the kind of men they were, of what we could do together, how it would be. How it would *feel*.

I wanted that. No inhibitions. My heart raced, my breathing was ragged, as if I'd run up the steps to the penthouse level. I ached for their lips on mine again, their hands touching me. I wanted to *feel*.

"I want the or," I said.

Their eyes narrowed, turned instantly hot and, all at once, I felt like prey. They approached slowly.

"The *or,* huh? Okay. Here's how this is going to happen, sweetheart." Ashe touched me first, his hand sliding up and down my arm, the caress gentle, but goose bumps rose on my arm. Seeing them, Sam went over to the thermostat on the wall, then returned.

"We're going to get you out of this pretty dress and see what's beneath. Delicate lace, maybe? I'm thinking black."

"No," Sam said, shaking his head slowly, his heated gaze raking over me as if he had Superman's x-ray vision. "Satin. Pink."

They were both wrong, but I wasn't going to tell them that. They'd find out soon enough.

"I bet you're nice and wet for us," Ashe continued. "That those panties, whatever color they are, are ruined."

I felt my cheeks heat as I nodded.

Sam grinned, then palmed himself through his

jeans. "Good girl, because my dick has never been so hard."

"This first time's going to be quick," Ashe added, ending the chatting by cupping my face in his hands and kissing me. Yes, *yes,* it was so good. The feel of his palms warmed me. So did his kiss. I wasn't cold any longer. I felt the pent-up need, the simmering arousal in Ashe's body, in how he kissed me. It was as if he had just crossed a desert and I was his first sign of water.

I felt Sam's hands on my shoulders, at my spine, the tug of the zipper and the slide of it parting my dress. Cool air caressed the skin he slowly exposed. Hands returned to my shoulders and slid the fabric off. It caught on my wrists, then slid whisper-quiet to pool at my feet. All the while, Ashe kept kissing me.

"Fuck, sweetheart," Sam murmured. I moaned when his palm curved around my hip before cupping my bottom. "White."

Ashe pulled back and glanced down, took in what Sam had revealed. "Gorgeous. Are you a virgin, sweetheart?"

My mouth fell open in surprise at the question. "I'm in a hotel room with two men. Not very virginal of me."

Sam's lips settled on my bare shoulder, kissed his way to the juncture with my neck. I angled my head to give him better access. "Friends of ours met their

woman and claimed her—her virginity, too—their first
night together."

"Friends?" I asked. Had I heard him right? Friends,
as in plural?

Sam's teeth gently nipped my skin, then his tongue
flicked out, soothed. "Jamison and Boone. One look at
Penny and they were done for. Turns out, she'd saved
her cherry just for them."

The idea of having my first time with Ashe and
Sam held appeal. They'd have made it so much better
than Jimmy Garcia in my freshman dorm, I was sure.

"Sorry, not my first time." I didn't think it was their
first time either.

"It's your first time with us. And, sweetheart, it's
your *last* first time."

I frowned, but Ashe kept going.

"After all the dirty things we're going to do to you
tonight, you won't be wearing white ever again."

After that, it seemed they were done talking
because Ashe's hands cupped my breasts and Sam's
hand slid around my front to my belly, then lower,
slipping beneath the lacy edge of my panties.

When his fingers slid over me, he groaned. But he
didn't stop, his fingers slipping right into me, nice
and deep.

I gasped, went up on my tiptoes.

"Tight. Hot. Wet. Perfect," he murmured.

The front clasp on my bra made easy work for

Ashe, the straps sliding down my arms, then to the floor as well.

"Perfect," Ashe murmured.

My head fell back against Sam's shoulder as he slowly fucked me with his fingers. In, almost out, back in. The sound of our ragged breathing, the wet slide of his fingers was all I could hear. I was sheltered and protected between them.

"Please."

"Ah, you beg so sweetly." Sam pulled his fingers from me, lifted them to his mouth and licked them clean. I looked over my shoulder, watching him do so. "You taste just as sweet. Fuck, Ashe, you need to have a taste."

"Gladly," he replied, dropping to his knees before me and putting his face right...there. Through the thin panties, he nudged me with his nose. His warm breath fanned my sensitive skin and I whimpered. My clit ached, swelled.

Hooking his fingers in the waistband, he tugged the delicate panties over my hips and off. I stood in just my heels while they were still fully dressed.

"I want to see you, too," I said, looking down at Ashe.

"Sweetheart, my dick stays in my pants until it's time to fuck. Otherwise, I'll come like a horny teenager all over those gorgeous tits." He grinned, but it slipped when he looked for the first time at my pussy.

I squirmed, but Sam's arms came around me, cupped my breasts from behind. Pressing close, I felt his heat, his hard muscles, and his hard cock against my bottom. I'd never really thought I was all that attractive *down there,* but the way Ashe was staring made me believe he felt otherwise. It was as if he'd never seen a pussy before, or my pussy was the most amazing one he'd ever laid eyes on.

Reaching behind my knee, he hooked it and lifted it up over his shoulder. Sam's hold kept me well balanced. "You'll come first, then we'll fuck you."

"I thought you said this was going to be quick," I breathed. With him hovering right in front of my pussy, I clenched my inner walls, aching with anticipation.

He looked up at me from between my legs. "Oh, sweetheart, you're going to come real quick."

And then his mouth was there, his tongue *there.* His finger, nice and deep...*THERE.* Between Sam kneading my breasts and his fingers tweaking and plucking at my nipples and Ashe's ministrations lower, I went from zero to sixty in about, well, sixty seconds.

My fingers tangled in Ashe's hair, my heel hooked into his back as I got hotter and hotter and...wow. White hot pleasure had me gasping, my hips curving and riding his face. "Yes, god, yes."

Ashe continued to lap as I came down from the incredible orgasm, and when he pulled away and looked up at me again—well, when I opened my eyes and looked down at him—he was smiling, very pleased with himself. His lips glistened. "That's one."

Oh, god, they were going to kill me with orgasms. My bones had melted from the pleasure, my fingers tingled, my skin damp with sweat. It was a good thing Sam had his arms around me as that was all that was holding me up.

Ashe lowered my leg then pushed to standing, began undoing the buttons of his shirt. I couldn't ogle at the exposed skin for long because Sam spun me about to face him, then kissed me.

I had no idea how long we kissed, but Ashe's words cut through the soupy fog of my brain. One orgasm wasn't enough for my body. It still hummed with desire and Sam's mouth on mine, his hands running over me, had my need returning for more.

"Come here, sweetheart," Ashe called from behind me. "Take my dick for a ride."

Sam lifted his head, smiled. "Better hurry. I'm pretty sure he wants to come deep in that tight pussy of yours, not his hand."

Turning around, I saw Ashe sliding a condom onto his very big, very long, *very* large cock. He'd ditched his shirt, shoes and socks and remained only in his jeans, which he'd opened and tugged down enough to free himself. It was one of the hottest things I'd ever seen. A man in just denim and muscles settled on a couch, legs spread apart, generous cock in hand.

He glanced at me, crooked a finger.

I crossed to him, put one knee on the couch and straddled his lap. Hovering over him, my breasts were right at eye level and he took advantage. Cupping my bottom, he leaned forward and took one of my nipples into his mouth. He drew on me in long pulls and I felt it zing right to my clit.

"Please," I begged again. I may have just come, but I'd been empty and now I wanted that cock deep inside me. Filling me up, easing the ache. The emptiness.

He pulled back, helped settle me over him, then slowly pushed me down. His eyes met mine, held, as I gasped. Fully inside me, I wiggled my hips, clenched and squeezed to adjust to him. I was stretched open, filled deep. He was so big. I was wet and prepared, but taking a cock like his wasn't easy.

"Fucking perfect," he murmured, settling against the back of the couch. He tilted his head back, watched. How a green gaze could be heated, I had no idea. But I'd felt those whiskers on the insides of my thighs, that mouth on my clit so wicked and skilled. "When you're ready, fuck yourself on me."

With his hands still on my hips, I lifted and lowered, finding a rhythm. He hit every hot spot inside me and my eyes fell closed, going where it felt good.

Moved how it made me hotter. Rubbed my clit to make me come.

"Look at her, so pretty. So fucking hot," I heard Sam say. "Do you like knowing I'm watching you fuck Ashe? I can see how his dick gets swallowed up by that dripping pussy. I can't miss the way your tits bounce, your nipples get nice and hard."

Sam kept up the dirty talk and it only made me hotter. It was thrilling, dark and dirty, having another man watch as I rode his friend. My hands went to Ashe's bare shoulders and he started to help me, lifting and lowering me, faster and harder until my head fell back and I came all over him. Ashe took over, thrusting his hips up into me as I rode the scalding hot waves of pleasure. I felt him swell inside me, his motions going from smooth to rough and wild as if his baser needs *finally* took over. He fucked into me until he thrust deep one last time, held still and groaned.

"My turn, pretty girl," Sam said, kissing my back as I lay slumped against Ashe's chest. I could feel his heart beating, could breathe in his musky, male scent.

After a minute, Ashe propped me up. I opened my eyes, grinned at him.

"Sam's turn," Ashe replied, the hard edges that I'd seen on his face now gone.

I nodded my head, knowing we were far from done. I wanted Sam, too. Two orgasms in and I wanted more. I wanted both of them. Without being with Sam, too, this night would be incomplete. I wanted what the two of them offered, as different as they were.

Sam's hands wrapped around my waist and he carefully lifted me off Ashe's cock, pulling me up. I hissed as I was spun about and tossed over Sam's shoulder. I laughed as the world went upside down. Sam's hand came down on my bottom in a light spank as he walked across the room and into one of the bedrooms. I bounced as I was dropped onto the bed.

As I propped myself up on my elbows, I watched as Sam stripped all the way. His body was solid and muscled, tanned and toned. Gorgeous. And that cock, the dark plum tone, the broad crown with the bead of pre-cum at the tip, the length. I licked my lips.

He must've seen where I was looking because he said, "Oh, sweetheart, you can suck me later."

Ashe came in the room, stuck his hand out and gave Sam a foil packet. Ashe must have disposed of his used one, then tugged up his jeans, but left the button undone. He looked disheveled, well-fucked. Virile.

"Thanks," Sam said, only glancing away from me long enough to protect us both. "That was two, sweetheart. Ready for orgasm number three?"

He didn't give me a chance to answer because he pounced and then there was no words except 'god' and 'yes' and 'harder'.

4

SHE

"YOU'RE GETTING me dirty all over again," Natalie said, her back pressed against the shower wall.

My hand was between her legs, feeling her wetness on her soft, warm flesh, and it wasn't from the hot stream of water falling on us. I slipped my fingers carefully inside her pussy, felt her tight heat. Fucking perfect. We'd been in her all night long and I would imagine her to be sore. Natalie had slipped from bed early to shower. As if I'd have slept through her leaving me; no fucking chance. I'd pulled back the white shower curtain and joined her, not being able to keep my distance, or my hands off her. Sam was asleep in the suite's other bedroom, but I knew once he got up, he'd want another turn, too. We weren't done with her, not ever.

My dick was hard, not going down even after fucking her two times. I had to assume Sam would wake up the same way. Horny as hell. We'd only hit the top few things on my fantasy list with her. It would take years...decades, to get through it all, and then we'd do it all over again. And again.

I grinned as I cupped her breast. I couldn't get enough of them. They were small, firm and were topped with little coral colored nipples that tightened so beautifully. They were very sensitive and when I gave one a little tug, I felt the clench of response around my finger deep inside her.

"I think we discovered last night that you're a dirty girl."

Her eyes fell closed as I found the little ridge on her inner wall that made her back arch, her eyes fall close. I knew just how to press, to curl my finger around her G-spot to make her come. But not yet. I wanted her on my dick when she did so. I loved feeling her orgasm, the way her walls all but milked the cum from my balls before I let go, filling the condom.

I wished we had no barrier between us when we filled her, that I could be in her bare, her sticky honey coating my dick like it coated my fingers, that my cum could mark her inside and out. But not yet. I knew her body, but a conversation about birth control had to happen before we ditched the condoms. And trust. I was clean, so was Sam, but while I was commanding her pleasure, she was the one in charge. She was giving us the privilege of her body and she said how. She said when. She said bare, and only then would we mark her officially as ours.

"Dirty? Only *with* you," she replied, her neck arching, exposing that long column of pale skin. "And Sam."

I leaned in, licked the water from her skin, kissed along her jaw to her mouth.

"Mmm," she murmured as I continued to tease her pussy. To tease *her*. "I've had fun with you guys."

Fun? That wasn't the word I'd use. Incredible. Insane. Amazing. Devastating, because life as I'd known it, my life before last night, before Natalie, was over.

There was no going back, and I didn't want to. I wanted her in my life, in my bed, my shower, hell, I wanted in her pussy forever.

"I'm sure I can speak for Sam and say we have, too. It doesn't have to end." I waited for her to open her eyes. "I don't want it to."

Her aroused gaze met mine. "It does. You're leaving."

I curled my finger. "And you're going to come."

"Come? Where? Montana?" she breathed as I stroked her G-spot with a touch more pressure.

"On my fingers"—I slid out and had a second join the first inside her slick heat—"and to Montana."

She frowned, but gasped when I nipped at the juncture of her shoulder and neck. Her fingers tangled in my wet hair. "Please, I want to come," she whimpered as I got her closer to the brink.

"Yes, ma'am," I said, working her expertly until she came all over my fingers, her cry of pleasure bouncing off the bathroom walls. The look of her as she did was the most beautiful sight. Wild, abandoned, completely uninhibited and open. Exposed. The real Natalie was revealed, and only for me and Sam. And right now, with the sounds of her pleasure bouncing off the steamy walls, all mine. *Mine.*

I slipped from her when she slumped against the wall, a little smile on her lips. With a hand on her hip, I held her up as it seemed her knees were a little shaky. To say I was proud that I'd made her all wilted and gorgeous was an understatement. She only made my ego grow...as well as my dick.

I wanted to fuck her, but I hadn't brought a condom to the bathroom. Didn't matter. My dick could wait, although it wasn't happy about it.

"What's this about Montana?" she asked as I grabbed the soap, began to slide it all over her. Fuck, Natalie's perfect body all dripping wet and slick with suds? It was going at the top of my spank bank fantasies.

I kept my eyes on her body as I spoke. "This wasn't the place to tell you this, the shower, I mean, but we're here to tell you that you've inherited a ranch in Montana."

She stiffened and her hands grabbed my wrists, stilled my motions. "What?"

I looked at her, saw the confusion in her eyes. All desire washed away, as if by the hot spray that fell on us.

"Your father, Aiden Steele, left part of his estate to you," I clarified.

She frowned. "My father?"

She slid back the shower curtain, the metal slide loud. Grabbing a towel, she wrapped it around herself, not taking the time to dry her body or her hair.

Shit. I fucked this up. I had no idea what her mother had told her about Aiden Steele. From the information we'd collected, we knew Natalie's mom had passed on three years ago of an aneurysm, so if she had kept it a secret, it had died with her. Her mother had married when Natalie was five, so it was possible she thought that man was actually her father. The way Natalie was responding, I had no idea what she knew. I *did* know I hadn't done this right. Sam was going to fucking kill me.

Reaching out, I turned off the water. By the time I

stepped out and grabbed a towel, she was out the door, cool air seeping in.

I found her by the bedroom window, looking out at the view. She'd tugged the curtains back enough to see, letting in a bright strip of morning light.

"What do you know about your father?" I asked. The air conditioning chilled my damp skin, but I didn't give a shit. I worried for Natalie.

She didn't turn to look at me. Her hair was darker wet and it dripped down over her shoulders, even onto the floor behind her. So beautiful, so close, yet untouchable.

"He died," she said finally. "A long time ago."

"That's what your mother told you?"

She looked over her shoulder at me. "Yes. Are you saying I inherited a ranch from someone who died over twenty years ago?"

Slowly, I shook my head. I proceeded cautiously, as if she were a skittish mare. "He died last year."

Turning to me fully, she crossed her arms over her chest, the slight swells of her breasts rising over the edge of the white towel. Backlit, it was hard to see her expression. "I think you need to start at the beginning."

"Let me get Sam in here." I walked to the bedroom door, opened it and called to him.

Within a minute, he came in, only having taken the time to slip on a pair of jeans. "What's up?" he asked, his voice rough with sleep. He took in Natalie in just her towel and grinned, walked toward her to kiss her, I assumed. She put her hand up, stopped him. If he missed the hand, her expression alone would have stopped him cold. "Ashe was going to tell me about my father. The inheritance."

All playfulness dropped from his face. "I see." He glanced at me as if trying to assess the situation, but finally nodded.

I went to the closet, grabbed the white robe off the hanger and handed it to Natalie. "You're cold."

As she wrapped herself in it, not dropping the towel to do so until after she was covered, I knew we were in big trouble. As she tugged the belt into a fierce knot, any chance of another round of wild sex was definitely over. While she was naked underneath, it could have been a full snow-suit she wore. We weren't getting to see any of her anytime soon.

I just had to hope not everything was over.

I sat down on the edge of the bed and told her everything. How Aiden Steele had died and left his ranch to five daughters. Four had been found and now lived in Barlow, but she was the last one. As I shared, she paced the room, listening intently.

"You're, what, investigators?" she asked finally.

Sam nodded. "We were hired by the estate's lawyer to find you."

"And you needed to do a full body cavity search to

confirm I'm the last Steele sister?" While the tone was all snark, she was serious.

Sam held his hands up. "Sweetheart, it's not like that and you know it. What we share—"

"What we share? What is it that we share? Are you this thorough with all your clients?"

"That's a low blow," I told her. "I think you know us enough to realize we're not like that."

She tapped her bare foot on the carpet. "Oh really? I find out I have a father I'd thought died over twenty years ago from two men I had a one-night-stand with and you think I'm the one tossing out low blows?"

She pointed to herself. Her cheeks were flushed and she was riled. Shit. *Shit.*

"You got what you wanted, to fuck me. Why toss these lies out now? You could just tell me to leave."

"Sweetheart," Sam said, the one word soft.

She narrowed her eyes, pointed at him. "Don't *sweetheart* me."

"We don't want you to leave. That's just it. We want you to stay. Last night was...amazing. You're it for us."

She laughed, but she shook her head, closed her eyes as if blocking us out. "It? Right. Look, I'll just go. That's what you want, right? No clingy goodbyes, no texting or stalking. No misguided woman wanting more."

She stomped into the living room and we followed. I

sat on the arm of the couch as Sam went into his room. She grabbed her dress from the floor, stripped out of the robe and stepped into it, working it up over her bare body. Sam returned by the time she got the zipper up at the back of her neck. I'd have helped, but I didn't dare get near her.

"Here." He held out her file, her paperwork. I could tell by the thickness that it was all of it, not only the details about the inheritance Riley had written up, but the information we'd collected on her. "This is everything."

She stared at the folder and it was obvious for the first time she thought we were telling her the truth.

"Riley Townsend's the executor of the estate. His information is on the first page. Call him."

"But...wait." She looked down at the carpet, deep in thought. Blindly, she went over to her heels, picked them up.

Sam afforded me a glance and we remained quiet, let her think. He still held the folder.

"Whatever's in that folder is one thing. But you guys picked me up *knowing* all this."

"I tried to tell you last night," I said. She'd asked us why we were in town and I offered to tell her, but she'd shut me down. And then I forgot everything altogether because I hadn't been thinking with my big head. Just my little one.

And look where that had gotten us.

Her eyes narrowed again. "You tried. You *tried?* Why didn't you try again?"

Shit, I realized I'd sounded all defensive and attempting to spin this back on her. No wonder we were still fucking single.

"This is a big deal. You were *following* me! Stalking me, even. I mean, you came to the restaurant, not my house or work. You didn't even *call* me. God, that's even more creepy than Alan."

I assumed Alan was her boss, and grudgingly, she was probably right. It didn't help the gut punch feeling, especially when we'd brought this on ourselves.

"One look, sweetheart, and you ruined us."

"Yeah, well, you ruined me, too," she replied. Her voice broke a little, but her spine was like fucking steel. Yeah, she was a Steele daughter all right. And not only did we fuck her, but we'd fucked up, too.

Balancing on one foot, she slipped on her heel, then the other. Reaching out, she tugged the file from Sam, then grabbed her purse and briefcase.

I stood then. "Wait, you're not leaving."

She spun and faced me. If looks could kill, I'd be dead. So dead.

"Watch me."

She went to the door in her day-old dress and heels, her hair wet ropes down over her shoulders. No makeup, no underwear.

She opened it and stormed out, the heavy metal making it slam behind her.

Running my hand over my face, I began to swear. The one and only woman we wanted in our life just walked right out. We forced her to do the walk of shame, which was like a kick to the balls to alpha males like us. We didn't make a woman do that, and not Natalie. Shit, not her. We'd hurt her deeper than I'd ever imagined.

And now she was gone. Out of our lives, all chances of something more completely gone. Dead. And it had been all our fault.

5

NATALIE

MONTANA WAS NOT what I expected. Well, I expected it to be cold, but it was *cold*. C.O.L.D. And it was April. Boston was cold, even occasionally snowed this time of year, but there was some kind of sharp bite I hadn't expected. Perhaps it was the wind that didn't seem to stop blowing since there weren't any trees to stop it. In my haste to leave, I hadn't packed a heavy coat, so I was wearing the one I just bought at the clothing store on Main Street in Barlow. With lots of puffy down, it was really cozy, but the woman at the store had also sold me a hat, mittens and sturdy shoes. As in cowboy boots. Where I'd been unprepared when I got off the plane four hours earlier, now I was over prepared, but at least feeling like I blended in.

I didn't. Not at all. I'd never been west of the Mississippi River and I'd never seen a real mountain. The Massachusetts's Berkshires didn't count. Now they surrounded me in my little rental car. Everywhere I looked, prairie, still brown from winter, patches of snow dotting the landscape. In the distance, the song *America, The Beautiful*, was right. Purple mountains majesty.

It was beautiful. And freezing.

It had been three days since I stormed out of Sam's and Ashe's hotel suite. I'd been so upset, so overwhelmed, I'd forgotten where I'd parked my car and had had to search two levels of the parking garage before I found it. If anyone had noticed my wet hair, they'd been smart not to comment.

I'd gone home and fumed. And hated men, two in particular. How dare they not tell me I'd been a job to them! How dare they not tell me the second they saw me that my mother had lied to me and my father had been alive for years and years. He'd even outlived her.

I'd never been close to Peter, my stepfather, so I couldn't say for sure if he knew about Aiden Steele specifically. He had to know my mother had been with *someone*. I looked just like her; I didn't come from a cabbage patch. While we didn't dislike each other, Peter wasn't the kind of guy to drop this kind of bomb on. If I didn't know about my father, then it was possible he didn't either.

It wasn't fair to him to share details I didn't even know or understand. I'd tell him eventually, but not right now. Same thing with my girlfriends. Since I'd texted Cara, my friend and neighbor, my location at Sam's insistence, I'd had to give her the dirty details of my one-night-stand, but that was all I told her. And I only mentioned one guy, not two.

I was embarrassed, mortified and confused. So I called the one person who could help me—without me wanting to strangle or jump him. Riley Townsend. As Sam had said, the lawyer's contact information had been on the top piece of paper in the folder. After reading through the details—most of which was about me—I had a long chat with the man.

And after swearing him to secrecy, I went online and booked a flight to Montana. Time off had been easy. It wasn't as if Alan had been able to argue with my request since I'd almost broken his fingers. He'd been low key, as if nothing more than a client meeting had happened, but had immediately signed off on my extended vacation.

Now, I listened to my GPS telling me turn in a half mile as I took in the north end of town. Small. Tiny. So tiny there was perhaps three stop lights. Boston, with its ridiculous traffic, was light years away. But Barlow was pretty. Quaint. The people were nice. Laid back.

They waved as they passed me on the road. The fact that I was recognizing that people were *nice* meant I needed to rethink where I lived.

Montana. Could I live here? As I put on my blinker, then turned left onto one of the neighborhood side streets, I tried to picture myself in Barlow. I'd need a whole new wardrobe. A job. God, a job. What could I do here? I had to assume the cost of living was much lower. It wasn't as if I couldn't afford it. And that wasn't even taking into account the inheritance. Riley had said flat out I was rich. A millionaire. If I were smart with my money and didn't buy a Lamborghini, I wouldn't have to work again if I desired. No more Handsy Alan.

But I could do that in Boston, too. The inheritance didn't require me to live in Barlow, although I could live on Steele Ranch. It was mine along with my sisters. God. I had four of them. And as I pulled up in front of an attractive home with a wide porch, I was about to meet one of them.

A sister. God. Besides Peter, I'd had no family since my mother had died. No grandparents, aunts, uncles, cousins.

But now, I had a huge family. Riley—and a guy named Cord—were married to Kady and they had a daughter. The other sisters were Penny, Sarah and Cricket, but I lost track of names for their spouses/significant others because none of them had just one man. They each had two, and from what I heard, Cricket had three.

It made me think of Sam and Ashe, how I'd had no issue with spending the night with both of them. Was it a Steele sister thing or what? I'd pushed thoughts of that night, of those two, down deep. Way deep, like buried in mud. Now wasn't the time to stew and drink more wine. I was in Montana meeting a long-lost sister.

My hands were damp inside my mittens and the car—and all the puffy clothing—felt suffocating all of a sudden. I was overwhelmed. Turning off the engine, I took a breath, then another.

Sam and Ashe wouldn't be here. I shook my head, as if I could shake those thoughts away.

The front door opened and a woman with bright red hair came out onto the porch. She wore black leggings, thick socks and a turtleneck sweater in a bottle green. God, she was pretty. Smiling, she waved and then curled her fingers.

I couldn't turn the car back on and pull out of the driveway. I was nervous, not rude.

Taking a deep breath, I stepped out, went up the walk.

"You look like you're freezing. Come inside," she said.

She closed the front door behind us and took my hat and gloves after I tugged them off.

"Just as I imagined. You look nothing like the rest of us," she remarked.

I shrugged out of my coat and hung it on a peg by the door beside a few others. Big men's coats and a shimmery silver one that had to be Kady's.

Boots were lined up on a mat beneath, so I assumed this was a no-shoe house. I toed off my new ones as Kady chattered.

"Penny's short and blonde, Cricket has darker hair but is taller. Curvier. But she has nothing on Sarah, who's like a pin-up girl." She put her hand to her hair and rolled her eyes. "Then there's me."

"I'm the one built like a boy then," I countered, looking down at myself in my jeans and long-sleeved t-shirt. In comparison to Kady, with her soft and lush new mother curves, I definitely had the physique of a boy. I'd dressed in my apartment when I got up this morning and now I was standing in front of a sister in Montana. Crazy.

"I bet Sam and Ashe didn't think you're built like a boy."

She grinned and I could feel my face heat. I looked anywhere but at her, took in the entry and the great room beyond.

"Oh my god." She grabbed my arm and stepped close. "You slept with them."

I glanced around some more. "How can you tell that?" I countered. Just then, a baby screamed from some other part of that house. "Don't you have to um... go see to your baby?"

She waved her hand through the air as if it were no big deal. "She and Cord are taking a bath together. Don't worry, that's not a bad cry. She's happy."

Whatever. She had that mother thing where she knew the various sounds her baby made and the DefCon status of each one.

"You slept with Sam and Ashe. I *knew* you'd get along with them."

"Get along?"

"They're sweet and kind and manly and drop-dead gorgeous."

"Who are you calling drop-dead gorgeous?" A man walked over to us, a smile on his face, easy demeanor. If Cord was in the bathtub, this had to be Riley.

He confirmed it. "Good to finally meet you," he said.

"You, too."

He was in jeans and a Henley, his fair hair a little wild as if he had yet to comb it today. Or Kady had been running her fingers through it. The way he pulled her into his side and kissed her temple, I assumed it was that.

"Sam and Ashe," Kady told him, putting her hand on his biceps.

"Ah," he replied, not adding to that. He was a smart man and he'd no doubt gleaned from my tone and adamant stance on keeping my being in town in secret that I didn't want anything to do with those two.

"Kady and Cord know you're here, but none of the others, as you asked," he said as if reading my mind.

Kady lifted her hands to the praying position in front of her, her big diamond ring catching the light. "Please, please let me call the others. We've been waiting for you."

"Waiting for me? I just found out about all this"—I circled my finger in the air—"just the other day."

"We've been waiting for our last sister for *months*."

I glanced to Riley who was smiling indulgently at his wife. "It's true. I never had sisters—brothers either, actually—so I can't say if they're any different than other families, but these four are really close."

"I'm an only child," I admitted, then shrugged. "Until now."

"It's true what Kady said, all four of them have been waiting for you, which means you're in trouble."

I frowned. "Trouble?"

"Please?" Kady begged, not answering my question.

I sighed, gave a small laugh, then nodded. "But just your sisters."

This wasn't that bad. The nerves I'd had since I stepped off the plane were gone. Riley was nice, Kady was ridiculously friendly and excited to meet me. Four sisters weren't Ashe and Sam. I wouldn't have to think about them at all or their trickery. How bad could four sisters be?

"YOU'RE NOT MARRIED, no boyfriend. So what's the scoop?" Penny asked an hour later.

As soon as I'd given Kady the go-ahead, she'd grabbed her phone and started calling. Instead of everyone—and I meant *everyone*—going to Kady, Riley and Cord's house, we'd gone to the main house at Steele Ranch. Penny and one of her men had been horseback riding there and it was agreed it was easier for so many people to get together in the big house.

They hadn't been wrong. There were fourteen of us, plus a few ranch hands. Together. Kady's rancher in town was a nice size, but this was like a Thanksgiving dinner. The Steele family had built a beautiful farmhouse back in the 1800s that had grown and morphed over the generations to be even bigger. I guessed five or six bedrooms, at least five-thousand square feet. Since our father hadn't claimed any of us, I had to assume it had been quite large and empty for just him. In death, he'd brought us all together.

Cricket lived in the house with her men, Sutton, Lee and Archer, and it suited them, especially since Sutton worked on the property and Lee, a professional rodeo rider, stabled his horse here. As for me? It was lovely but way, *way* out in the boonies.

It had taken ten minutes more for Sarah to show up from the town library, sharing that she'd closed up early just for me. Cricket and Boone had arrived a few minutes later in scrubs, having come from the hospital, although it had been quickly clarified they weren't together. As in *together,* especially since Cricket greeted her three men—and not Boone—with very thorough kisses. Thirty minutes after that, Penny came with Jamison from the stable. Boone was the third of *that* group. Two ranch hands, Patrick and Shamus rounded out the party.

I'd lost track of who belonged to who after that, completely overwhelmed. All I knew was the head count.

Four new sisters and nine brothers-in-law! Plus two ranch hands.

And now I was in the kitchen surrounded by all four of my sisters. I sat on a high stool at the peninsula part of the counter, three of them on one side, one on the other. It wasn't a sneak attack, but darn close. And the questions...gah. All four of them were eyeing me, waiting for my answer to Penny's very direct and personal question.

While Penny had a baby on her shoulder and she was patting his little butt in a blue striped onesie, she had the look of a woman out to get the 411.

At least the men weren't in the kitchen. In the great room, the TV was on some sport and they were talking, although I couldn't hear—or process—what they were saying. Kady, Penny, Cricket and Sarah were all staring at me, waiting.

Oh yeah, Penny's question. "The scoop?"

While we all shared the same father, none of them looked the same, just as Kady had said, but they rolled their eyes in sync.

"No husband," Penny said.

"No."

"No boyfriend," Sarah added.

"No."

"Yes to Ashe and Sam," Kady tossed out.

"What?" Cricket said, her voice almost gleeful. "They are gorgeous and need a woman."

Kady leaned on the counter so she was closer to me, the others leaning in as well. "She slept with them. And by *slept,* I mean they didn't sleep at all. Right?"

$\mathcal{N}$ATALIE

I FELT my cheeks heat as I stood up and went to the fridge with my empty glass. I knew I was a guest, but I wasn't going to just sit there and be interrogated, especially on such a touchy subject. Why they were so eager to learn about my night with Ashe and Sam was surprising. I was a brand-new sister. Didn't they want to know about my bra size and the type of shampoo I used? I found the pitcher of iced tea and refilled my glass.

"I bet they were good."

"Are you a thing now?"

"Where are they? They must be so glad you're here."

After shutting the fridge door, I turned to face them. They leaned against the counter, wide- eyed, waiting for answers to their peppered questions. "Do you only do this to the new sister? Hazing?"

Kady put her hand on her chest. "I was first. I had to deal with Cord and Riley all on my own. Then there was the bad guy and the murder and my other half-sister and—"

My mouth fell open as I listened to her.

"I was second," Penny said, cutting her off. "Kady wasn't much help because when I showed up, she wasn't even in town. I had to deal with the whole losing-my-virginity thing on my own."

"Jamison and Boone certainly helped," Sarah countered, reaching out and patting baby Locke on the back.

"You're one to talk," Penny countered. "Wilder and King refused to even take off their pants until you married them."

Sarah bit her lip to keep from replying, but from the bright color of her cheeks, Penny wasn't tossing out wild accusations.

"Which took what, two days from when you guys finally got your heads out of your asses after a decade and got together?" Cricket asked. She turned to me. "I'm the slut of the group. I had a one-night-stand with

Sutton at a rodeo and he pulled in Archer and Lee. Let's just say it was a weekend-long one-night-stand with three guys. Then I left them."

"But you're here," I replied, knowing there was a lot unsaid. Their stories were interesting, and hilarious.

"Long story short, I was put in sheriff department handcuffs, brought to Steele Ranch and fucked," Cricket added.

"Oh," I said, taking a sip of tea. One of her men, Archer, wore a sheriff's uniform, so I had to assume the handcuffs belonged to him. I had no idea how to respond. "I want the long story long. All of it. And that murder thing Kady blurted out."

"Oh no," Sarah said, holding up her hand. "It's your turn, sister. We want the dirty details. The dirtier the better."

I glanced from one to the next. Kady, with her red hair and pretty clothes. Penny, all petite and blonde with the sweet little baby. Cricket with her spunky attitude and sly smile. Sarah with her long black hair and killer curves.

"How is it there are nine men out there and they're not bothering any of us? Aren't they thirsty or anything?" I asked.

"They are well-trained." Sarah narrowed her eyes. "And I see you are skilled at evading. This is what happens when you arrive last. Four sisters to torture you."

I bit my lip, torn between liking the feeling of them so interested in me, but also bothered, as if they were poking an open wound with a stick.

"I don't like them," I replied simply.

"Ashe and Sam?" Penny asked, frowning. "Why not?"

I took a deep breath, let it out. "Because they told me after I slept with them who they were, that they'd been investigating me, had an entire folder on me."

They stared, and stared some more. Penny's hand even stopped patting the baby.

"They didn't tell you who they were? Like made up fake names and stuff?" she asked.

I shook my head. "No, they were truthful about that, but the next morning, I was...well, in the shower with Ashe and he just spit out that I was an heiress and he was in Boston to tell me that."

Sarah blinked. "That's awful, but I'm stuck on the mental image of Ashe in the shower."

Kady laughed. "Me, too!"

"You're not bothered by it like I am?" I asked, surprised by their lightheartedness.

Cricket came over to me, tugged me across the room so I was in front of them again. "If you hate them, we hate them, too. We're on your side."

They all nodded and Sarah pulled me in for a hug. She was so much shorter, so curvy and in a few decades, would make a perfect grandma giving some sugar. "The jerks."

I laughed then. *That* wasn't sugar, but it felt good knowing she had my back. "I felt...embarrassed. Used. Tricked."

The words came easier now.

"Yeah, the jerks," Penny added. "But I've known them for several months now. They've never behaved that way that I've ever seen."

"Ashe drove me to the hospital when my water broke," Kady admitted. "I'd been at home and I called the office. Riley was in court with Cord so Ashe came right to the house. He took the turn into the driveway on two wheels. You would have thought he was the dad. He was completely freaking out."

It was hard to imagine, the Ashe I knew had seemed to be so...chill.

"Maybe they just screwed up," Cricket added. She cocked her head to the side, studied me. "I mean, look at you. You're gorgeous. Any guy would be thinking with his dick at the sight of you. And those two? Yeah, you might think they're dicks for how they revealed everything, but I bet they have really big ones. Dicks, I mean."

I laughed then. Fully. "Yeah, they do."

All four of them laughed and hollered, whooped it up and gave each other high fives.

"What did they say when they apologized?"

Kady asked.

"They didn't." I held up my hand when they looked ready to go after them with pitchforks. "I mean, I didn't give them a chance. I was so upset, I stormed out of the hotel room. I haven't seen them since."

"Well, I heard Cord say they were back in town. Why not let them have a chance to explain?"

"Yes, Natalie, why don't you let us have a chance to explain?"

Kady, Sarah, Penny and Cricket whipped around at the sound of Sam's voice. The baby made a funny whimper/burp sound at the jostling and Penny started patting his butt again.

My heart lurched, skipped a beat and then started racing at the sight of him. Sam. God, he looked good. Better than I remembered. Bigger. Broader. More… chiseled. He didn't even afford the other women even a glance, his dark eyes squarely and solely on me.

"Sam, um…hi."

"Me, too," Ashe said, moving into the doorway to stand next to Sam.

Oh, god, the full effect of the two of them could still ruin my panties, even after hating them for the past few days. My mind might be wanting to strangle them, but my body wanted to climb both of them like a tree.

"How did you find me?" I asked. I didn't think Riley would have said anything. He'd be a terrible lawyer if he had.

"You two are jerks," Penny said, stepping in their way. She was a foot shorter than both of them and the way she had to tilt her head back to yell, the effect was lost. Especially with a baby on her shoulder. "And how *did* you find her?"

They didn't look at Penny, but at me. Her being so short, it was a clear view. But Cricket stepped behind her and so did Kady. "If you're in trouble with our sister, you're in trouble with us."

"Flight records. It wasn't a big leap to think you'd come see Riley, then end up here," Ashe admitted.

Kady had her hands on her hips and Cricket's chin was tipped up, listening. "That was smart," Kady admitted. "But you're still jerks for upsetting our sister."

In that moment, everything came into sharp clarity as if things had been out of focus and I'd put on some glasses.

My sisters were standing in front of two big guys, protecting me. It was like I was on the elementary school playground and they were blocking me from a bully. Or two. I'd never had anyone do that for me in my life, and these women? I'd only known them for about an hour. Yet they were ready for a WWF smack down with Sam and Ashe.

I laughed, hiccupped, then began to cry. And I wasn't a good crier. In fact, I was a hot mess when I cried, splotchy face, swollen eyes, lots of snot, but I couldn't help it. I couldn't stop it.

Hands patted my back and I was pulled into a chest, hugged. Grandma Sarah and her big bosom.

"See? You've upset her."

I cried even harder at the way Sarah snarled at the men.

"What the hell is going on in here?" I recognized the voice as Cord's, which was as big as he was.

"Ashe and Sam made her cry," Kady said, sounding just like a little kid tattling. It made me laugh, the sound a weird mix of a sob and a snort, which had to be extra unattractive to Sam and Ashe. But it wasn't them that had made me lose it. Well, them partially. It was that I had four sisters who were like mama bears protecting their cub.

Before Ashe and Sam were dragged out back and beat up, I stood upright, wiped my face and moved away from Sarah.

"Better?" she asked, eyeing me with concern.

I nodded. "You all just met me and are ready to march those two out to the woodshed."

"You're our sister," Cricket replied, as if that answered it all.

"But you've known them longer." I cocked my head toward the duo. "You said you liked them, that...that they were your friends and still, you believe me, stood up for me."

"Honey, look at them," Sarah prompted.

I glanced at Ashe, who had his shoulders slumped, his head angled down and watching me cautiously through his thick lashes, and Sam, whose hand was running over the back of his neck as if ready to climb out of his skin.

"We know them, yes, but they're men," Sarah continued. "They're stupid and often think with their dicks, like Cricket said. That night in Boston, were you thinking with your dick, Ashe?"

"Yes, but can you blame either of us? Look at her," he replied.

"See?" Cricket said, crossing her arms over her chest.

"Our first glimpse of you, we were ruined," Sam admitted. "It's like the other guys in this house. Cord here, for example. When did you know Kady was the one?" he asked, glancing to the side at the big...BIG man.

Cord grinned, eyed Kady. "The second I laid eyes on her in the baggage claim. She hadn't been in town five minutes."

"We wanted you, sweetheart," Ashe said to me. "*Want* you. We weren't keeping our reason for being in town a secret, nor your inheritance. It's just that we wanted you more."

"You," Sam added. "Right then in that bathroom hallway when we first talked to you, your father, the inheritance, all of it had been irrelevant, our job, too. Then in the hotel room, all that mattered was making you come."

The women sighed and Cord slapped Sam on the back, grinning.

I flushed hotly remembering just how they'd done that. And more than once.

Sarah put her hand on my arm. "We'll still think they're jerks if you want. But they're Barlow men. They know what they want and go after it. Ask my guys. Once we figured stuff out, I was married to them two days later."

I flicked my gaze to hers and she held up her left hand, showed me the rings Wilder and King had given her.

"I got pregnant my first time," Penny said.

"The coffee table in the other room," Cricket added. "Let's just say Lee, Sutton, Archer and I defiled that thing. And sanitized it after."

"Come on, sweetness," Cord said gently to Kady. "I think Ashe and Sam can take it from here. Besides, Cecily's going to wake up hungry any minute."

"But—"

"Let them get to the good part," he replied.

I kept my eyes on Ashe and Sam.

"The good part?" she asked, taking his hand and following him into the great room.

"Make up sex."

7

AM

"I NEED to get in you, get you to come all over my dick, then we'll talk."

We'd driven to my house back in town and I'd held her hand as we went inside, but that's as far as we made it. I had her up against the door, unzipping the coat that kept me from all her soft curves.

"Sam, I—"

I stopped her words with a kiss. The first kiss since Boston, since *that night*. I'd been pissed and cranky ever since knowing we'd fucked up. While I'd tried to tell her the truth and she'd shut me down before we even got our clothes off that night, I was smart enough to know never to tell a woman it had been her fault because, well...I liked being alive. And it wasn't all her fault. It wasn't as if she'd expected us to tell her we were investigators, that we *had* been stalking her in the restaurant.

She probably thought we were car parts salesmen from Tulsa or even cattle ranchers from Montana. Whatever. Just not the truth. I should have insisted, held my dick off until we'd told her everything. But she'd been just too perfect. We'd wanted her too much. Like now. Now, I had her in my sights, had my hands on her, could breathe in her citrus scent, hear her ragged breathing. Even tasted her in the kiss. She was right there with me, right there with Ashe by our side.

"Sam, no."

I stopped, pulled back immediately at that one word, but not too far. Her dark eyes slayed me. Heat and interest were there, but so was doubt.

"I want this," she said. "Both of you, but we need to talk. This was our problem last time. I should have given you the chance to tell me everything that night. Or the next morning. I should have stayed. Listened, instead of running away."

"And we shouldn't have let you do the walk of shame," Ashe added. "We're sorry, sweetheart."

"You want to talk?" I asked, pushing her coat off her shoulders. Ashe took it and hung it on the coat rack beside the door.

"I think it would be best," she admitted, placing her palms flat against the door at her sides. "I mean, we've slept together and I don't even know your last names. Where you went to college. Whose house this is."

Glancing down her body, I could see she was eager. Not just for information, but for us. She looked so good in that simple shirt and jeans, completely different than the dress from the other night. I had to wonder—so did my dick—what lacy confection she wore beneath.

She was more than her lingerie, more than the soft feel of her skin, the heat of her pussy. One of the things that was so attractive about her was that she was smart. Brilliant, even, but we'd barely talked with her. While it made me proud of myself to have reduced her to saying single syllables like 'yes' and 'harder' and 'more,' I wanted words. Lots of them. I wanted to know about her, too. Her likes and dislikes. I wanted to hear her opinions on things, to debate and possibly even argue—although not about how Ashe and I had fucked up.

"All right," I agreed, then grinned. "You ask a question and we'll answer. In trade, we get a piece of clothing."

She arched a dark brow. "Strip twenty questions?"

I grinned. "Sure."

"I have more questions than clothes," she countered.

"We'll do our clothes, too, right, Ashe?"

"Hell, yes."

"I still have more questions than all our clothes."

"Sweetheart, haven't you figured it out by now?"

Natalie's frown got even deeper. "What?"

I couldn't resist, I reached back and tucked her hair behind her ear, felt the silky softness between my fingers. "We've got forever to learn it all."

She cleared her throat. "Forever?"

Ashe came to stand right beside me, shoulder to shoulder. "This isn't a one-night-stand. We want it all with you."

"All?" she squeaked.

"Sweetheart, we must have really messed up if you don't know how we feel," I added. "We want you. Only you. We knew the first time we saw you. That's why we fucked up. We were too damned eager for you."

"We have control now," Ashe added confidently. "Maybe just a little. So ask your questions."

"And you get the clothes?"

I shook my head. "The clothes go on the floor. We all get answers and we all get naked."

I saw the curiosity and the heat in her dark eyes, but we waited. She'd said no and we wouldn't touch her unless she wanted it. *This. Us.*

She toed off her shoe as she asked, "Do you guys have family? Parents, brothers and sisters?"

"My parents live about a mile from here," I offered.

Only a shoe came off, but it was a start. "My dad owns the mechanic shop on Main Street and my mom's a radiologist at the hospital. One brother. He lives in Denver."

"My parents live in Portland. No siblings."

His parents were retired and liked to travel. It was hard to keep up with their adventures; they were either in Machu Picchu or the Galapagos this month.

"My turn."

She nodded.

"Are you a sports fan?" he asked.

Her mouth fell open and she glanced between the two of us before she spoke. "You aren't those crazy sports fanatics who break up with a woman because she likes the wrong team, are you?"

Ashe shrugged as he began to undo the buttons on his shirt. I reached behind my neck, tugged my Henley up and over my head.

Her eyes went to our chests as she responded. "My stepdad is a big fan of hockey. When I was little, I watched it with him. It's probably the only real thing we share, and a dislike for the Red Wings. Penguins fan, here."

That was hot. A woman who liked hockey. Worked, since Montana was frozen more than half the year. Lots of hockey to watch, at least on a club team or juniors level.

"How did you get fixed up with Riley?" She toed off her other shoe.

"We actually run our own IT company. Security." I angled my head into the house, but the basement was the business's office space. "Ashe and I met in college and we sold our first company a few years later. I wanted to come back here, to Barlow, and Ashe followed. Started another company, one to keep us from getting bored. We don't actually work for Riley, but occasionally for Cord. We do some investigating, online searches, stuff like that for him. But you—or at least the last Steele daughter—were hard to track down, so he asked for our help."

"Then we saw your picture and knew we had to be the ones to tell you about your inheritance," Ashe added.

I ran my hand over the back of my neck. "We blew that, didn't we? But shit, sweetheart, you're too hard to resist."

"We wouldn't let anyone else have you," Ashe finished, toeing off his shoes.

"I didn't ask a question," Natalie said, pointing to the way Ashe kicked his shoes out of the way.

He shrugged. "I'm not shy, sweetheart. I'll answer naked."

"My question, sweetheart," I said. Her gaze was level, her demeanor calm. Good. "Why do you work for that asshole?"

She pursed her lips, as if she were eating a lemon, or thinking about how much a dick her boss is. "I like the industry."

"You mean you like lingerie," Ashe countered.

"I do. I like to wear it because it makes me feel pretty...feminine. It's not for a guy, but for me."

"You took the job because you like lingerie. That's good. Being in a field you like is good. But why stay? You can just go to the mall and get sexy little scraps of lace..." I ran my hand over my face thinking about what was beneath her white shirt. Pink? Lavender, maybe? Satin? "Why stick around when you're sexually harassed? There are all kinds of jobs with your skill and background."

She gave a slight shrug. "It hadn't been too bad, until recently. That night at the restaurant, that was the worst. I'd been thinking about switching jobs, but now...well, now I have a lot to decide."

Being an heiress certainly helped with options. She could continue to work for the asshole—although we'd certainly try to talk her out of it—or another company or not work at all. Hell, she could become a llama farmer if she wanted. She could do anything she wished with that sharp brain of hers.

But not today. Not now. We'd be there for her no matter what she decided, but now I couldn't help dropping my gaze to her chest. "You're wearing something skimpy and sexy now?"

She nodded. "I wasn't expecting a guy...or guys to see it. Like I said, I wear it for me."

"You wear it for us now, too," I said. "Show us."

"Yeah, sweetheart, put us out of our misery."

She gave us a sly glance, then put a hand on the wall for balance as she removed one sock, then the other.

"Cruel, woman. Very cruel," Ashe said, slowly shaking his head. He palmed his dick through his jeans.

"My turn," she said. "Where's the bedroom?"

Fuck yes.

I held out my hand, just like I had that night in the restaurant. She glanced at it, then me. Took it. Giving her warm palm a little squeeze, I led her through the family room and up the stairs, down the hall and to the master bedroom.

"This is your house?" she asked as I flicked on the light just inside the door.

"I live about a mile from here," Ashe added. His house had acreage. As he'd grown up in Portland, one of his requirements for moving to Barlow had been a view and space. No close neighbors. It wasn't anything like Steele Ranch with the thousands and thousands of acres, but he had room to breathe.

While I liked my house, my home was now with Natalie, wherever the hell she was. If that meant moving to Boston, so be it. If she wanted to live in Ashe's house here in Barlow, that was fine, too. I'd live there with them. Or, we could find something that was new to all of us. I didn't care as long as she was in it. But that was added to the growing list of things that didn't matter right now.

"I think you have to take something off," she said, eyeing us both.

We were both shirtless at this point. Neither of us wasted time in shucking our jeans so we stood before her in our underwear. Ashe had on black boxer briefs, I had on navy boxers.

She paused, ogled, her eyes growing wide at the way my dick tented my boxers.

"You're so smart, sweetheart," Ashe said. "Do you think we'd be here with you if we didn't want you? All of you? For the long haul?"

"I..." She licked her lips. "I just don't understand why you want *me.*"

Ashe glanced at me and I nodded.

"We should spank that ass."

"What? Why?" she asked, stepping back.

"Because you think so little of yourself. Fuck, woman, you're smart. You're successful. You light up the room. Hell, you light us up. On top of all that, you're sexy as fuck."

"Love at first sight, Natalie," I said simply. "The heart wants what the heart wants."

"Love?" she said, staring at me as if I'd just admitted we were aliens instead of in love with her.

"That's a question," I said with a wink. "Take something off."

She stared at me for a second, then gave me a sly look. Her fingers hooked in the hem of her shirt and she lifted it, revealing creamy skin one inch at a time. Slowly, so fucking slowly. When pale blue fabric appeared, both Ashe and I groaned. And when she lifted her arms over her head to remove the shirt entirely, I practically came in my pants. She wasn't wearing *just* a bra. It was one of those...fuck, a bustier or whatever. The name was irrelevant. There was about three inches of lace beneath her breasts, then see-through mesh of the same color that cupped her small curves, the nipples plainly visible and hard.

"Fuck," Ashe growled.

She grinned now, broadly, as if she felt empowered by our responses.

"You can bring us to our knees, sweetheart," I told her, ensuring she knew how perfect she was.

"You like this?" she asked, sliding her palms up over her the fabric around her ribs, then higher over her breasts.

"We like your brain, too. Not that you can tell right now," Ashe said. "Like Cord said, we're currently thinking with our dicks. Lingerie seems to have that effect."

She giggled and I loved the sound. "So what would happen if I conjugated Russian verbs as I took off my jeans?"

My hand stilled over my dick. "You speak Russian?"

She glanced up at me through her dark lashes as she popped the button on her jeans. "Yup. Did a college semester in Moscow."

"You're going to make me come," I told her. Brains and beauty. I was ruined.

It was completely silent in the room as she took off her jeans and stood back up, solely in the pretty blue bra and matching thong. She didn't have crazy curves, but she was lithe and lean, toned and everything I ever wanted.

She took a step, then another, toward us. And to make my balls boil, she dropped to her knees before us, licked her lips. "Yes, you are."

8

ATALIE

I BELIEVED Sam when he said he loved me, the look in Ashe's eyes that proved he felt the same. Insane, really, since I barely knew them. But that was normal world ideas. Normal world time. It seemed Barlow time, or perhaps Steele sister time, was different. Faster.

Meeting Kady, Penny, Cricket and Sarah, I realized how different we were. We looked nothing alike. Our personalities were so varied. Yet we were also *very* similar. We each fell for multiple men. I knew no one who'd done the polyamory thing. Until now, and then they were all my sisters. And me.

As for the guys, they were all ridiculously male,

very alpha and extremely focused on their woman. They had similar caveman traits as Sam and Ashe. Possessive, protective and ridiculously in love. They, no doubt, wore the pants in their little family units, but the women ran the show.

From their stories, each of them had fallen head over heels in love with their men immediately. Love at first sight. Wham!

That was why Sam and Ashe had been such dumbasses in Boston, because they'd seen me and fallen in love with me. I'd made them lose their minds.

And *that* was very powerful.

And even now, being on my knees before them, I was still powerful. The sight of Sam's dick, all hard and pulsing for me, so eager pre-cum beaded at the slit...I made him this way. I'd reduced him to a Neanderthal. *Must fuck and plant seed. Must get inside woman. Now. Grunt. Grunt.*

I reached for Sam's dick and he moved his hand away, pushed his boxers down so they slipped to the floor. In my hold, he was hot and smooth, yet hard as steel beneath.

"You can suck my dick, sweetheart, but I'm coming in that pussy."

Ashe didn't delay, but dropped his boxer briefs so I had two cocks before me. I'd seen them before, *felt* them, but hadn't had a chance to look this closely. They were both big. Thick. Long. Curved so they reached toward their navel. Heavy balls hung below, large in their virility and need for me. But they were different, too. The hair at the base was different color, the flesh on Sam's was a ruddy red, Ashe a touch pinker. Sam's crown was flared, Ashe's not as blunt.

My mouth watered, ready to do a taste test.

I licked up that pearly drop from Sam's tip, the salty essence of it bursting on my tongue. Turning, I gripped Ashe with my other hand, tasted him, too. Muskier.

"Fuck, sweetheart," Sam murmured. "Look at you."

I swirled Ashe's flared head like an ice cream cone, then took the tip into my mouth, sucked on it. Just that part of him made my mouth open wide, my lips stretch.

Ashe groaned, then hissed, then he stepped back, gripping it himself. I watched as he pumped once, then came, his cum spurting out thickly, landing on my chest and belly, marking my sky blue longline bra.

Seeing him come, to watch the pleasure on his face, the hard look of almost agony as his balls emptied, was so fucking hot.

I shifted, my pussy aching. There was so much cum, it was obvious he'd been saving it for me.

On a rough breath, he grinned. "Shit, sweetheart, you've ruined me. And your pretty bra."

"If it made you come like that, I'd say the bra did its job."

His cheeks were flushed, but I wasn't sure if it was

because of just coming or because he was embarrassed. I stood, reached up and cupped his jaw, felt his dick, still hard, pressing against my belly. "You still want me or are you done?"

His eyes narrowed, heated at my blatant dare. "Done? Sweetheart, with that load blown, I can fuck you all night." He stroked my hair back from my face. "Tell me, have you ever had a guy take your ass?"

I squirmed at the thought of it. "No, but...I'd like to try."

Ashe's fingers tightened in my hair at my response, then he kissed me.

Sam came to stand behind me, felt the heat from him as he put his hands on my shoulders.

Ashe pulled back, caught his breath.

"Are you on birth control, Natalie?" he asked, moving his right hand down to my arm so he could kiss the spot where my neck met my shoulder.

"Yes, the pill."

"Good," Sam added. "Since you're not fucking anyone else ever again, I think it's time we take you bare, don't you?"

Not fucking anyone else? That meant...he really meant...right then and there, between the two of them, safe and protected, I felt...loved.

I bit my lip, then grinned, went up on tiptoe and kissed Ashe. His cum had cooled and I felt it smear on his bare chest, but didn't care.

"I've never done that, always used condoms, but yes. God, yes."

Ashe smiled, very pleased.

"I'm the one who suggested it, sweetheart," Sam murmured. "Why does he get all the attention?"

Ashe arched a brow and I turned around, faced Sam.

"That's right. I was on my knees but you never got any attention, did you? Poor baby."

I stroked my hand over his hair, let my fingers tangle at the nape.

He wrapped his arms around me, lifted me up and carried me to the bedroom. Tossed me onto the bed where I bounced, then laughed. "Spread those legs, sweetheart. Let's see that pussy. I want to see where my dick is going...bare, as soon as I know you're ready."

Sam was almost feral, his cock even bigger than before, pre-cum slipping down the length in one slow stream. He was on the edge and I didn't want to tease him any further. Teasing him meant teasing me because I wanted that big, needy dick in me. Now.

And so I bent my knees, spread my legs wide, then reached down and pulled my thong to the side so they could see me.

"If you like that little scrap of lace, take it off, or in five seconds it'll be in shreds on the floor."

"I work for a lingerie company. I've got drawers full of pretty things."

Sam just growled in response. While the idea of him ripping my panties off was, in itself, hot, I did like this set and so I lifted my hips, pushed them down and with my toes, flung them onto the floor. Forgotten.

Like Ashe had been, I was on edge, and they'd barely touched me. If either of them put their mouth on my clit, I'd come. To move things along—since Sam said he wanted to make sure I was ready before he fucked me and I *really* wanted that big, glorious dick filling me up—I slid my hand down my belly and over my pussy, coating my fingers. I held them up, showed them how *ready* I was.

Sam moved quickly, grabbing my wrist and lifting my fingers to his mouth, licked them clean.

"A dirty girl, aren't you?" he asked, when done.

"A *ready* girl. Fuck me, Sam. Bare. Be my first."

He growled, then moved on top of me, nudging my legs wide so he could settle between them. His cock slid over me, getting coated in my wetness before notching into place.

His eyes met mine. Held.

"I meant what I said, Natalie. This is love. This is everything."

He pushed in, one big, thick inch at a time until his hips met mine, his balls bumping my ass. I clenched and squeezed to accommodate him and I pushed up to take him deeper.

"Yes," I breathed.

He paused for just a second, then his control snapped.

He fucked me with ruthless abandon, deep and hard, the slick sound of it filling the room along with our ragged breathing.

I hadn't known my eyes had fallen closed until my nipple was pinched. Ashe grinned as he played with one, then the other after pushing the bra cups down, all the while Sam fucked me. Neither stopped, neither let up until I came, then came again.

While Ashe had been the one to come, Sam had the stamina to make me whimper and all but beg for him to come, too. I wanted to share how good it was between us.

And when he finally did, our skin was slick, my body was lax and my mind fuzzy with too much pleasure. He stiffened, held himself still as he groaned. Harsh lines of painful pleasure slashed his face. I could feel the heat of his cum as he filled me with it, as it slipped out around him to slide down to the mattress.

It was too much, too good.

But we weren't done. For Sam pulled out and sat back on his heels, watched his cum slip from me. Ashe reached behind my back and deftly unhooked my bra. I helped him take it off and he tossed it over his shoulder.

"My turn. You rode my lap in Boston. It's time I take

you for a ride," Ashe said. "And see how much you like ass play."

Sam moved out of the way as Ashe flipped me onto my stomach, pulled me back and up so I was on my knees, my head resting on the bed. "This is the first time I've ever gone without a condom. I can't wait to mark you, nice and deep. Ready, sweetheart?"

I nodded and I moaned as he slid deep. "Fuck."

I groaned, the new position having Ashe slide over completely new, very sensitive places.

"Here," Sam said, but I didn't know what he was talking about. But when I heard a lid pop open and felt the cool dribble of liquid on my back entrance, I knew what Ashe's plans were.

He kept up the slow and consistent pace of his hips, fucking me in a cadence that had me getting closer and closer to coming. But when I felt a finger brush over me *there*, all slick with the lube, I gasped, clawed at the bedding.

God, the feeling was electric. Intense. Combined with him deep in my pussy...

"Like that?"

"Yes," I breathed, closed my eyes and just *felt.*

"Good girl," he murmured. His free hand went to my hip, gripped. The slap of him against me the only sound in the room. That and my whimpers as he pressed a little more firmly at my untried hole, trying to gain entrance, although my body was naturally fighting him.

"Shh, relax, breathe."

I did. Breathed and focused on not tensing up. This caused the tip of his finger to slip in me. I moaned, clenched.

"Shit, sweetheart, you're squeezing my dick."

He rode me then, fucking me as he slipped in and out of my ass. Not any deeper than that initial entry, but that was enough. God, when he pulled back, it lit up nerve endings I didn't even know existed and I came. Hard. Like really, really hard and I screamed, wanting more. I pushed my hips back, met him thrust for thrust.

All at once, his control was gone. While he'd removed his finger from me, the feelings lingered. He took me, harder, faster and deeper. Longer and longer still until I came one more time. Only then did he finally come, filling me just as Sam had, marking me inside and out with his cum.

Right here, with them, I was home. Filled with them, my body and my heart.

"If I didn't know you just rode a horse for two hours, I'd think Ashe and Sam broke you," Cricket said, slowly shaking her head and laughing at the way I was walking up the path. She stood on the porch of the main house at Steele Ranch watching me as I gingerly made my way up the walk. She held baby Locke in a football hold, his chubby little hand shoved in his drooling mouth.

It had been two days before either Sam or Ashe had let me up out of bed. I hadn't minded as I'd been just as insatiable as them. We'd spent the time fucking, definitely, but also talking, getting to know the things we should have perhaps before the wild night in Boston. But it seemed normal convention didn't really work for us and we had our first real date in Sam's bed and without clothes.

With the text messages and voice mails piling up about a girls' trip to Bozeman to go shopping, I'd finally told the guys we had to make an appearance at the ranch, otherwise my sisters would show up and start banging on Sam's front door. Neither was too excited about that—their showing up at the house part —because his house was our sanctuary.

But my sisters could be held off for only so long. Besides, the guys had work to do. I'd originally come to Montana to find out about my inheritance—since I'd hated Sam and Ashe then—but now it was also to get to know my sisters. I hadn't told HR how long I would be away from work, but right about now, I didn't really care. The office and handsy Alan were two time zones away.

Sam and Ashe had brought me to Steele Ranch just after breakfast. When Jamison—not only Penny's husband but also ranch foreman—heard I'd never ridden a horse except at summer camp, he'd insisted playing tour guide and led a ride so I could see the land I'd inherited. The weather was warmer, at least for the moment, with the sun shining...and thankfully no wind. Penny had wanted to join, making up for the time she hadn't been able to while she'd been pregnant, so Patrick had helped Jamison get five horses ready to go.

After a two-hour leisurely ride, I'd dismounted, bowlegged and sore, but nothing worse than when fucked by my men. Which was the reason for Cricket's joke.

I glanced at Sam. He was smart enough not to say anything, but smiled nonetheless. Leaning in, he murmured, "If you aren't walking like that after we fuck you, we're not doing it right."

Ashe laughed. "When you get home later, if your ass and thighs are still sore, I'd be happy to rub them down."

I whimpered at the thought of a massage, and what Ashe would do after.

"If you keep talking like that, I won't be going anywhere with the girls," I replied.

Ashe leaned in and kissed me.

"Hey! None of that," Cricket called. "Kady's on a

mission."

Ashe pulled back, ran his knuckles over my cheek. His eyes held heat, promise and humor. "Go, have fun."

Sam spun me about, kissed me as well. "Not too much fun."

They walked to Sam's truck and left.

I glanced at Cricket on the porch. "Like I said, I think either Sam, Ashe or the horse you rode in on broke you."

I went up the walk, stepping gingerly. My inner thighs were quivering from hugging the horse's flanks and my ass was still numb from the saddle. "Yeah, not only do I obviously lack endurance for a horseback ride, but for fucking two men non-stop for two days," I grumbled.

She wrapped her arm around me and led me inside. "You should take three guys for a spin."

Three? God, I could only imagine the kinds of things she got up to with Sutton, Lee and Archer. My pussy all but whimpered at that much attention.

"Sarah and Kady are already here," she continued. "After you and Penny shower and she feeds little Locke here, we can head out." The baby shoved his hand greedily into his mouth. She'd played babysitter while Penny was riding with us.

I groaned. "A hot shower sounds fabulous."

"Don't take too long, Kady's eager to get to the mall."

"I am!" Kady shouted from somewhere inside the house. "The weather's shifting and the men want us back before dark. If you're not ready to go in thirty minutes, I'm dragging you to the car."

"She will, too," Cricket whispered. "And Penny will have to nurse Locke by lifting her shirt and leaning over the car seat."

God, it felt good to have sisters. A family. Kady cared enough about me now to annoy and pester me, to have experiences with each other like somehow, and in some way, nursing a baby in such a weird way. If that wasn't a sign of a close sibling bond, I didn't know what was.

9

ATALIE

I'D DRIVEN from Bozeman to Barlow the day I came from the airport. It was a good thing since I was somehow driving all of us home after our day of shopping. They'd all had wine with our early dinner. I'd taken a muscle relaxer to alleviate the pain in my ass—literally—and so I'd skipped the alcohol. They weren't drunk, especially since Kady and Penny were nursing, but I'd readily volunteered to be the designated driver.

Kady's SUV was huge. A tank compared to my compact car, which was perfect for Boston's narrow streets and parking. And driving the behemoth felt like steering a tank about; soft turning and heavy on the brakes. But, it was high off the ground and fit five women and two car seats with the three rows of seating.

We'd left the highway behind and were thirty minutes from Barlow on the two-lane back road. It led up and over a mountain pass with twists and turns. Kady had been right, the weather had turned, especially at the higher elevation. The road was wet from rain mixing with snow and I worried they would get slick.

"You look like you're concentrating for your driver's test," Sarah said.

She was in the passenger seat beside me, Cricket and Kady in the back seat with Cecily in her car seat between them, Penny in the third row with Locke's car seat beside her.

I loosened my grip on the wheel at her words and offered her a small smile. I hadn't even realized I was leaning forward until I took a deep breath, relaxed. "I'm not used to these roads." I angled my head toward the back. "And we've got precious cargo."

Sarah put a hand to her chest. She wore a white blouse with a spring colored yellow cardigan. She looked like the prim librarian, but when I saw the outlines of nipple rings through her bra when we'd been trying on clothes, I had to assume she wasn't as prim as she appeared. At least with Wilder and King.

"I'm not precious cargo?" she asked, grinning.

"We all are," I replied. "I think Aiden Steele was a dumbass."

That earned a snort from Cricket. I flicked my gaze to the rearview mirror, saw her roll her eyes.

"He obviously missed the safe sex lecture in school. I mean, didn't the guy know how to use condoms?"

She had a point.

"I think he was a lonely man," Kady added. "Never married. From what Jamison said, always lived alone in that big house. He had five daughters. Five! He at least knew of you, Sarah, but chose to not have a relationship with you. With any of us. I think it's sad."

I slowed the car around a turn. The sky was leaden with heavy clouds, light snow falling. It was just after six, not close to dark. Visibility was good, but this was a mountain road. Steep drops, sharp curves, lots of animal crossing signs.

I'd learned Sarah had been the only one of us to grow up in Barlow. She'd known Aiden Steele was her father and he'd never once approached her. This blew my mind because while Peter wasn't the best stepdad in the world, he *had been* there for me. Dinner at six every night. He'd even interrogated Ethan French when he'd picked me up for my first date in eleventh grade. While Sarah seemed relatively fine with being ignored as she had been, I could only imagine she had some serious baggage to go with it. From what she said, everyone had been surprised, including Wilder and King, of her parentage when she'd finally told everyone back in the winter. While I doubted the others would divulge any secrets, Sarah was a vault.

"Yet he brought us all together. Kady's right, it's sad he had to die to accomplish it," Penny added. "I'm not saying I would have liked him much, but knowing he was out there until last year makes me feel like I missed out on getting to know him."

Locke fussed and then settled. I hadn't heard a peep from Cecily and had to assume she was asleep. That girl seemed to like the vibrations of the SUV and had conked out the entire way to Bozeman. Of course, as soon as the car stopped, she screamed bloody murder because she was hungry. Kady had stayed in the car and nursed her before joining us in the mall.

"You just have to decide to stay," Sarah said.

I relaxed into a short straightaway before a sign indicated a left curve up ahead.

The others fell silent and I knew they were all staring at me.

Stay in Barlow.

Sarah didn't mention Ashe or Sam in her statement, but it was a given. If I were to stay, I'd do so with them. Although, if I ended up hating their guts, my sisters would still want me to remain and I knew they'd have my back.

I hadn't made any decision about moving to Barlow

and I hadn't really talked about it with Sam and Ashe. The two had barely let me out of bed enough to get a snack let alone consider relocating across the country. We were tight. The bond we shared was really, really good and well, I'd fallen for them. Hard. If I admitted it to myself, I fell for them from the first time I saw them, just as they'd said it had been for them. Love at first sight.

It was just this...thing that loomed, but was being ignored. Especially by me.

"That's right," Kady added. "Then we can all be together. A big family."

The idea was appealing. It felt...good to have each other, to see Cecily and Locke and know they'd be more than just cousins. With all of the Barlow men being so dang virile, I had to assume the two babies wouldn't be my only niece and nephew.

It made me think of having a baby with Ashe and Sam. It was crazy, but possible. Not right this second since I was on the pill, but I had no doubt when I went off them I'd be pregnant just by them looking at me. I squirmed, thinking of the guys, and the fact that my ass was still sore. All of this, even the numb butt showed me what it could be like living here. What my life could be—

Bam!

The sound of a tire blowing was loud. A pop or a deep boom, but the SUV shook violently and I was glad I'd been gripping the steering wheel because it jerked. Hard.

Sarah's palm slapped the dashboard and gasps came from the back and I couldn't even think about that. Instinctively, I put my foot on the brake and we swerved. My boring-as-hell winter driving lessons with Peter kicked in and I pulled my foot off the brake a bit, knowing we'd skid and I'd overcorrect. How I thought all that, I had no idea. It was as if time had sped up and slowed down all at once. Instinct took over.

Tires skidded, screeched and I was thankful there wasn't a passing car.

"Oh shit." We were headed for the guardrail, the only thing that separated us from the steep rocky edge. It wasn't a cliff, but if we went through it, it was going to be bad.

So I intentionally overcorrected, turning my wheel sharply to the left. The front turned into the mountain, but the back of the SUV slammed into the guardrail, bouncing us off and across the road.

I slammed on the brakes, the anti-lock kicking in with a grind and we skidded about fifty feet to a shaky stop. Sarah's head whipped forward and our seatbelts caught us. We were diagonally in the road, but on the wrong side. It was obvious now the front left tire had blown, since the SUV dipped down in that direction.

My heart was in my throat and I was sweating.

"Is everyone okay?" I asked, glancing at Sarah, then

turning to look in back. Penny, Kady and Cricket all nodded, but they looked scared as shit. Kady and Penny were leaning over the car seats, soothing the babies, although neither made a noise. I had a feeling they were just relieved they were fine.

A vehicle pulled up and a man climbed out. I unclicked my seat belt, hopped out. Other than my soreness from the morning ride, I was fine. Shaky, but fine. The man was in his fifties, his pickup truck a dually. He was dressed for ranch life and had a rifle resting in a gun rack in the back window. He had salt and pepper hair, a full beard. I assured the guy we were all unhurt, but we took in the damage to the SUV.

A late model truck slowed to a crawl, a car-crash looky-loo. I barely gave the driver a glance since the man who'd stopped to help was talking to me, but I did a double take. Had that been—

"Let's call the state patrol," he said, snapping me out of my thoughts. The truck was gone and we were still with a flat in the middle of the road. The back end smashed. "You'll also need a tow truck."

"There are five of us in the car," I told him. "We all have cell phones, so we can make the calls."

Sarah climbed out and I heard one of the babies crying, then was silenced when she shut the door, most likely to keep the heat in.

"Did you hit an icy patch?" he asked, walking over to the flat tire.

It was cold, the snow falling. It wasn't hard enough to stick, but the road was wet.

"No. Or, I don't think so. It wasn't like I slid and caught the tire on something. It just blew."

He leaned down, studied the tire, then stood.

"It's shredded. Strange, because the tread is good."

"I called 9-1-1," Sarah said. She'd put on a coat and handed one to me. I hadn't even realized I was chilled until then. "I also called Archer. Cricket said he was working today."

Archer would know who to call, what to do. I didn't know about jurisdiction between agencies, but I did know our men. They'd be here in full force soon enough.

"Did someone—"

"Cricket called Sam. They'll be here soon."

I let out a breath, felt the adrenaline rush still. God, I was used to dealing with things like this on my own. I hadn't had a tire blow before, or nearly gotten five women and two babies killed by driving off a cliff, but I'd been alone for a while. Knowing Sam and Ashe were coming made me realize in that moment that I *always* wanted them to come. To be there for me.

10

SHE

WHEN SAM'S CELL RANG, I'd expected it to be Natalie, to say they'd decided to spend the night in Bozeman, or were late returning because they'd had too much fun shopping.

"It's Cricket," he said, frowning as he answered the call.

A second later, I hadn't expected the look on Sam's face, or the way he'd stood up, knocked his chair over. We were at the diner on Main Street with Jamison and Boone and as Sam reacted, Jamison's cell rang. He knew it wasn't going to be good and put the phone to his ear. "Kitten," he murmured, glancing at Boone.

Sam looked to me and Boone as he hung up. "A tire blew. Cricket said they're all fine, but they're up on Culver Pass."

Shit. That pass was infamous for accidents. Bad ones where cars have slid through the guardrail and over the steep edge. The incline was enough where if something went over, it kept going until it hit bottom, hundreds of feet below. Brakes had gone out on the west side of the pass enough where a runaway truck lane had been built.

The SUV they'd driven was big and had the latest safety features, but ice or snow, a runaway tanker truck or even an animal cutting across the road in front of them might be too much for it.

"Why isn't Natalie calling us?" I asked. Grabbing my phone, I called her, but she didn't answer.

Boone pulled out his wallet, tossed a bunch of money on the table without even counting it. We were out the door within seconds, Jamison still on the phone. All I could think about was Natalie and why she wasn't picking up. I was reassured Cricket said they were all fine, but I doubted I'd be satisfied with that answer until I saw Natalie—all of them—myself. At least hear her voice.

Sam fished out his keys. All four of us climbed into his big truck and he pulled out into traffic. It was almost impossible to go only twenty-five through town when I wanted him to floor it.

Shit. *Shit!*

Natalie's smile, the feel of her skin, the sound of her laughter filled my head. I loved her. We'd only just found her and I wanted her forever, not have her taken away from me within a week.

The other women, too. If something happened to them—

I turned off the radio so we could listen to Jamison's side of the conversation and so I could try Natalie again. He'd gotten confirmation that no one was hurt, the babies were perfectly fine. That had eased all our minds, but I could only imagine how Riley and Cord were panicking, but Penny had said they were talking with Kady, too. The tire blew on a turn and the car stopped on the wrong side of the road. A passerby had stopped to help, had put his hazards on and laid out flares.

"Ask Penny why Natalie's not answering her phone."

After a few seconds, Jamison said, "She's out of the SUV talking with a guy who stopped to help."

The panic that was like a vise around my heart loosened just a little. Just having him talk with Penny made me feel a little better. She was fine. Scared, but unhurt. Locke was fine. She was our connection right now since Natalie was busy and the other women were most likely talking with their men. She'd tell us if something changed, if any one of the women or Cecily somehow became injured. Sometimes a wound became apparent after the adrenaline wore off.

Mine hadn't. I wouldn't feel better until I saw all of them, had Natalie in my arms. Hell, I wouldn't feel better until I had her home, naked, so I could look over every inch of her. Then fuck her. Hard, so I knew she was with me, well. Fucking whole.

I tried her cell one more time, then tossed mine on the center console.

I glanced at Sam, knew he was thinking the same thing, that we wanted to hear her voice, to just *be* there, but I didn't want to distract him. His jaw was clenched, his grip tight on the steering wheel.

Once we were past town limits, Sam gunned the engine. We knew the sheriffs in town and from what we heard via Penny, they were on the way as well. Archer, especially, since he was working today.

Jamison passed the phone to Boone. As an ER doctor, he asked pointed questions about seatbelts, bruises, loss of consciousness, airbags and other things I'd never considered. But since he'd waited until after Jamison talked, I had to guess it was more for his peace of mind than lifesaving. But then I remembered that Cricket was a nurse. She was smart and had a level head on her shoulders. She wouldn't have been calling Sam if she had to give first aid.

It took only twenty minutes to get to the women, not thirty like it should. We pulled onto the shoulder and I hopped out before the car was in park. There were two state patrol cars as well as a sheriff's SUV, which I assumed was Archer's. Red and blue lights flashed. There was a lot of manpower for a blown tire, but we were on the curvy pass and I had to assume it was going to snow harder up here as soon as the sun went down and the temperature dropped. No one wanted another accident.

The SUV was just as Cricket had said, facing the wrong way and on the wrong side of the road. I could see the blown tire from a distance. The back end was smashed in as if it had scraped along the guardrail.

Then I saw Natalie talking with Archer. My heart lurched, then settled. Fuck yes. There she was.

I all but ran to her, Sam a few steps behind since he'd had to turn off the truck. Out of the corner of my eye, I saw Jamison heading toward the SUV. Penny flung open the door and jumped into his arms. Boone went past them and leaned into the truck, most likely to check on Locke.

Natalie turned, saw us, and walked toward us. Her eyes were wide, her cheeks pale and her chin lifted. But as soon as we got within ten feet, it started to wobble.

Hell.

She looked whole, but when I pulled her in for a hug, felt her soft, strong body, breathed her in, I knew the truth of it.

"Fuck, sweetheart. You scared the shit out of me."

"Me, too." Sam stood beside us, ran his hand over her hair.

"Yeah, well, I scared the shit out of me, too," she added, then burst into tears.

I cupped her head, pulled her in tight. Leaning down, I kissed the top of her head and just held her. All around us, things were happening. Boone carried Locke in his car seat toward Sam's truck. Sutton's SUV pulled up with another right behind. He, Lee, Riley and Cord piled out of the first, Wilder and King from the second. None looked happy, their eyes taking in the scene, searching for their woman. I knew the urgent feeling.

Boone pointed toward the SUV and they headed that way, long legs eating up the distance. I could see the women within, most likely staying warm and out of the way. And Kady with Cecily. Jamison had his arm wrapped around Penny and followed Boone. A tow truck pulled up, the engine rumbling, diesel fumes filling the crisp air. A state patrol officer waved him closer.

So much was going on, but all I cared about was Natalie. The guys were all here and could take care of their own women.

When her crying jag tapered off, she pulled back, wiped her face. "Sorry, I guess the adrenaline bled off."

Sam pushed her hand away and wiped the tears

himself, then took her from me. Hugged her. "That must have been scary. Pretty amazing driving."

She laughed. "My stepfather taught me how to drive. Forced me to learn how to handle the snow, bad weather and rough conditions. At the time, I hated every second of it, but I guess I need to call and thank him."

Archer came over and looked from Natalie to me. I nodded, telling him she was doing okay. He didn't look too happy. His hands went to his hips. "You said the tire just blew out, Natalie?"

She nodded, then pointed. "Over there, just before the turn."

I could see skid marks on the road behind the SUV, saw where she'd been aiming when she turned into oncoming lanes. I could see there was nothing beyond the guardrail, that if they'd gone over, they'd all be dead.

Archer's jaw clenched and he held something up.

I frowned. "What the fuck is that?"

It was a small piece of dark metal with three spikes. A weird triangle.

"A caltrop. A tire spike."

Natalie took it from Archer. It was small enough to fit in her palm.

"Careful. They're really sharp," he warned. "I found it down by where you said your tire blew," he added, pointing around the bend.

"What?" Sam all but shouted. He stepped away, went around in a circle, rubbed the back of his neck. "Are you saying that was in the road?"

Archer took it back from Natalie, shrugged. "I only found the one and it was on the shoulder. It could have been there for a while. Who the fuck knows."

"That isn't a teenage prank," I added, pointing at the spike. Cops used it to stop car chases.

Natalie stilled. Her breath puffed out in little clouds. "I didn't see anything and I was focusing really hard on the road, too. It was snowing like this." She glanced up at the gray sky, the light flakes. "Not too hard, but lower down it was raining. Being from Boston, I know how to drive in bad weather, but I've never driven such a big SUV. God, that thing was really hard to stop."

Archer gave her a reassuring smile. "You did good. Real good."

"She's been out in the cold for a while. Can we get the ladies out of here?" I had no interest in remaining a second longer than necessary. Archer knew where to find all the women if he needed to question them. Hell, he had one of them in his bed. elThe state patrol could handle the tow truck. As for the SUV, I didn't give a shit about it. I doubted the other men did either.

"Definitely. Why don't we all catch up tomorrow at the main house?" Archer asked. His radio squawked. "I think we're going to all need some quiet time with our women."

I glanced at Sam, who nodded and shook Archer's hand.

I readily agreed, then took Natalie's hand, walked to Sam's truck. The guys were carrying the last of the shopping bags and coats from the damaged SUV, loading them in the back of Wilder's ride. The women and babies were tucked into the three vehicles. We were all free to go. I had no interest in seeing this section of road ever again.

Sam pushed up the center console and I helped Natalie in so she sat between us in the front. I didn't want her any further away and I secured her seatbelt myself. In the backseat were Penny and Boone, the car seat between them. Penny was looking down at Locke, smiling as she gave him a pacifier. Boone nodded and Sam didn't wait any longer.

We drove back to town. I held Natalie's hand the whole way. I didn't think I would ever let go.

11

NATALIE

I STARTLED, gasped and my eyes flew open. For a second, I didn't know where I was, taking in the dark room, trying to figure out how my bedroom window ended up on the wrong wall, that the door to the bathroom was on my right. Then it came to me. I wasn't in Boston in my apartment. I was in Sam's bedroom. Montana.

He was curled around me, his front to my back, an arm flung over my waist. I felt his even breathing at my neck, his bottom arm my pillow. I was safe. Warm. Cozy. Even so, my mind wouldn't let me settle into deep sleep. They'd brought me home, fed me, showered with me, fucked me. It hadn't been gentle, but frantic. I wasn't even sure how or why they'd waited past getting through the front door before they were on me. But they had. And they'd been on me for two hours, taking me more than once. They'd been hard and ready for me, but even after coming, they *still* had needed to sink into me, touch me, kiss me, just as much as I'd wanted them. To know I was alive, to feel the pleasure that came with being together. It had finally soothed me, put me to sleep.

But now I was awake once again. The clock on the bedside table said four. I could hear the rain outside the window and knew dawn was a long way off. I felt their cum between my legs, so much of it, still slick and sticky as it slipped from me. I ached deep inside; they weren't small men. I smiled to myself, one of pure feminine satisfaction. I had two lovers who were voracious, eager and very talented in pleasuring me. Just me. They were gorgeous and no doubt women flung themselves at them all the time, and yet they wanted *me*. Sam was holding me now, Ashe in the guest room asleep.

"You okay?" Sam murmured, his voice rough with sleep. He stirred, slid his hand up and down my arm.

"You're a light sleeper," I replied.

He kissed the back of my neck. "Not used to having a woman in my bed."

I gave a small laugh. "I can't believe that."

"I'm not a monk, sweetheart, but you're the first woman who's ever been in my bed."

I stilled, thought of what he said.

"You mean—"

"You're the first woman I've ever brought home. The first I've ever wanted here. I love holding you like this."

"What about Ashe?" I had no idea about being with two men on a relationship level. Sex with two guys, it was pretty obvious what they wanted. But when we weren't fucking, were they jealous of each other? Did Ashe feel left out by being in the other room?

"I'm sure he loves holding you, too." He kissed my nape again. Gently. "You're ours, Natalie. I think we've made that clear. We want you. We want you in our beds. For the long haul. We haven't talked about you going back east, but you have to know we want you to stay. And if you do, you get both of us. If you'll have us, that is."

"I...earlier on the pass, I knew you'd come, that I just had to wait for you to show up and everything would be better. That I wouldn't have to deal with that alone."

He slid back, turned me so I was on my back and he loomed over me, propped up on his elbow.

"Ah, sweetheart." He leaned down, kissed my lips. Once. Twice. His fingers moved to my hair, brushed it back, again and again, soothing. I knew him to be tender. Sweet, even, but he'd never been like this. The blown tire had really made us all sensitive and vulnerable.

"You might go off on your own, but we'll always find you," he murmured.

I felt it, knew it to be true. They were investigators after all. And it felt good. Sooooo good, as if, well, as if I were precious. That I was wanted. Needed, even. My heart was full.

"As for Ashe? He'll have to speak for himself, but you're his, too. But you can be his and be with me, like this. Sometimes you'll be with him. And sometimes, like earlier, we'll be with you together."

I didn't say anything, just considered his words. We hadn't talked about me staying. We hadn't talked about my job or my life back in Boston. I had yet to decide, so I'd just kept quiet. Being here, being in Sam's arms, in Ashe's too, like earlier on the side of that miserable road, was incredible. I'd fallen for them. Hard and fast. But did that mean I could leave my life in Boston behind? It wasn't like I'd had too much time to think about it. And right now, I didn't want to.

"Want to talk about it?"

"What, exactly?" I asked. Staying in Montana? The accident? Being with two men? How I'd fallen for them? And we hadn't even mentioned what brought us together in the first place. Aiden Steele's inheritance.

"Anything." The feel of his touch was comforting. "What woke you? Did you have a nightmare?"

I gave a slight shrug of my bare shoulder.

"Maybe. I don't remember. Just...unsettled."

While it was dark, I could see his face, his worried eyes. Lifting my hand, I cupped his jaw, felt the rasp of his beard.

"Those four, no...five orgasms we gave you earlier weren't enough?" he wondered.

I felt his smile against my palm.

His playfulness relaxed me, but his words made me eager. My body was responding to his being pressed against me. Every naked inch of it. And his cock was hard against my hip. I'd never had sex like this before. Explosive, steamy, wild. My body craved it.

I shook my head, bit my lip.

"Our girl is greedy for our dicks, huh?" he asked, stroking my hair back from my face.

His dick pulsed against me and I felt the wet heat of pre-cum as it spurted onto my side.

"You're just as needy as me," I countered, shifting so I could reach for him, grasp the base of his hot length and slide my fist up and down.

He hissed, his hips bucking.

"You need both your men, don't you?" His voice had dropped an octave.

My hand stilled and I looked up at him. I did. I wanted Ashe, too. I wanted to feel surrounded, to feel four sets of hands, and two dicks. Definitely. But then I worried.

"Ah, sweetheart. I can read your mind. I'm not bothered you want Ashe, too. We'll call him in and give you what you need, then in the morning, maybe I'll slide down the bed and wake you up with my head between your thighs. You know I love to eat your pussy. And knowing we've been at you all night, that our cum still fills you up..."

He groaned and I got wet.

"Ashe!" he shouted. "Get in here, our woman needs another fucking."

"Sam," I groaned, embarrassed. Turning my face into his chest, I breathed him in. Soap and sexy man.

But when, seconds later, Ashe came through the doorway, naked and very aroused, I wasn't embarrassed any more. Nope, my mouth watered to get at both of them again. Insane since it had only been a few hours. I was a total Ashe and Sam slut.

Ashe fisted himself, stroked from base to tip. The corner of his mouth tipped up. "You need more of this?"

I sat up, let the sheet fall to my waist. "Yes, but...but I want to be in charge."

Ashe's hand stilled as his eyes dropped to my chest and he grinned. He came around the bed, slid in beside me, laid flat on his back so I was in the middle, putting his hands behind his head. "I'm all yours."

Yes, he was, every delectable hard inch.

Sam shifted into the same position as Ashe and I swiveled about so I faced them both. Two naked and very aroused men on either side of me, cocks aiming upward. My pussy clenched in anticipation.

"Wait," Sam said leaning up and gently placing a hand over my eyes. "Close them for a sec."

I did and I felt the bed shift, then the colors behind my eyelids. He'd turned on the bedside lamp. Slowly, I blinked, let my eyes adjust. It was a soft light, not too bright, but I could definitely see them now. And they could see me.

"Much better," Ashe said. "I love seeing our girl as she rides our dicks."

I blushed.

"After what we've done together, you're still shy?" he asked.

I glanced away, shrugged. I was kneeling between them. They could see everything, my hard nipples and a hint of my pussy.

"But you want us at your mercy?"

I met his green gaze. "Yes. You're both so...bossy. Dominant. It makes me lose my mind and then I can't enjoy seeing your faces when you come. I can't see what makes you hot."

"Sweetheart, everything about you makes us hot," Sam added. "Trust me, you can't do anything we won't like."

"You want to suck us?" Ashe asked.

I blushed again, but the idea held appeal.

"How about sitting on my face?"

My eyes widened at the possibility. "I've never...I mean—"

Ashe grinned and his cock got harder, pulsing off his belly. "Oh, that makes you hot. Since we can't touch you, straddle me and climb up here. I want a taste."

He moved his arms down and by his sides out of the way.

I wanted this and having him verbalize it all made it easier. It was one thing for me to throw a leg over his waist and crawl up his body so my thighs were by his ears, another to say I wanted to ride his face.

"Grab the headboard," he instructed.

I did.

"Now lower down. Good girl, just like that."

"Oh!" I cried as his mouth latched on and his tongue found my clit.

My fingers clenched Sam's headboard.

"Don't close your eyes. Look at me," Sam said.

Turning my head, I met his dark gaze, saw the heat there. He was looking at all of me and I could only imagine what I looked like.

"You're gorgeous. I love the way your hips are rocking. I bet you didn't even realize you were fucking yourself on Ashe's face."

I was. Oh god, I was totally using Ashe and he

wasn't touching me anywhere except for his lips and tongue.

"Your tits are swaying, bouncing as you move. Every line of you is gorgeous. Want me to play with your ass? Get both your men on you?"

I whimpered.

"She just got wetter," Ashe said, his hot breath fanning my pussy.

I heard a drawer open, the flip top on a bottle of lube, then the slick feel of Sam's fingers against my back entrance.

Between that gentle touch and Ashe's tongue flicking my clit, I came. Toe tingling, mind blanking bliss.

My slippery hands released the headboard and I carefully fell to the side onto the mattress, not able to stay upright any longer.

"I was supposed to be in charge." I pouted, but it was hard since I felt so dang good.

Ashe wiped his mouth with the back of his hand, then shifted so he was lying on his side, his head propped up on his elbow. He looked well pleased with himself.

Sam moved, crooked his fingers. "Another time. Now up on your hands and knees. I want to play with that ass. One of these days, sweetheart, we'll take you together. But you have to be ready first."

I tingled...back there, from his finger and I wanted

more. How did a woman know she liked butt stuff? And when she did, how did she get through sex without it? I had no idea, but I didn't want to find out. I'd come once, but I wanted more. They were right. I was greedy.

And when the two of them put their hands on me *everywhere*, I knew they'd make me forget about everything until I was too exhausted to care.

 AM

"Everyone is so going to know what we did all night," Natalie murmured as I helped her down from the truck. We'd just pulled up in front of the main house at Steele Ranch for lunch—a very late one for us. She had on a pair of jeans and a sweater, but wore her cowboys boots she'd gotten the first day she arrived. They looked damned good on her, as if she belonged here. She did. She might have been born a city slicker, but Aiden Steele's genes were a part of her and this land was her home.

"Sweetheart, I'd bet my right nut they were all doing the exact same thing," I told her.

She looked up at me and frowned, then laughed. "I happen to like that right nut."

I swiped the tip of her nose with my finger. "Good to know."

Natalie had finally fallen asleep around six—we'd made sure she'd practically passed out from pleasure —and didn't wake up until an hour ago. Based on the fact that it was after noon and the trucks parked out front, I assumed we were the last to arrive.

Cricket and Sutton met us out on the porch. The weather was milder today, the storm having blown off overnight, and they left the door open behind them. Sutton was one scary looking guy. He'd even shot point blank and killed a fucker who'd been after Kady. He hadn't blinked an eye at it, and since last summer when it happened, he didn't seem to regret it at all. Riley and Cord had, because they'd wanted to be the ones who took the guy out. With his close-cropped hair, tattoos and intensity, most people steered clear of Sutton. Cricket, however, had softened him. While I didn't dare say that to his face, he'd probably agree. Our women were the best things that had happened to all of us. I gave Natalie's shoulder a squeeze, for my own comfort and peace of mind instead of hers.

"You might not want to go in there," Cricket warned, thumbing over her shoulder.

We stopped on the top step, Ashe right behind us.

"Why?" Natalie asked.

"I'm not fucking that pussy without a condom for two more months." A voice shouted from inside. My eyebrows winged up at the very private words. Was that Boone?

I glanced at Sutton, who was slowly shaking his head, then at Cricket, who grinned.

"Penny is ready for another baby." Sutton wasn't one for many words, and his single sentence response explained it all.

"But I'm ready now. The doctor gave the go-ahead," Penny countered.

"*I'm* a doctor and I say your body needs longer to recover. Tell me, kitten, are you picking a fight with me about this because you need my dick?"

It was quiet. Penny didn't respond. I felt wildly uncomfortable for unintentionally eavesdropping. Cricket and Sutton acted as if this happened every time Penny and her men stopped by. Ashe and I had been to a few get-togethers with the group, but this was a first.

"Is it always like this?" Natalie asked.

Cricket laughed. "They don't usually argue, but someone—or two someone's—"

"Or three," Sutton cut in.

"—usually has a quickie in the office or laundry room."

"I heard about the quickie on the coffee table," Ashe countered.

Sutton looked his way, face serious. "That wasn't a quickie."

I laughed, trying not to imagine what Cricket with her three men did not-so-quick in the great room.

A door slammed inside.

Cricket angled her head. "And there's today's quickie—with condoms."

Sutton tugged Cricket back in the house now that the argument was over.

Natalie looked to Ashe, then me. "You're not planning on dragging me off to some room for sexy times, are you?"

"Sexy times?" I loved that term. I tucked her hair behind her ear. "Do you want that?"

She shook her head, the wayward curl falling forward once again. "Everyone knowing we had sex last night? Fine. But I'm not getting it on just down the hall."

She wasn't an exhibitionist. Duly noted. I'd fuck her anywhere she needed it, including the laundry room, but I wasn't bothered if it didn't push one of her hot buttons. She was a wildcat in private and that worked for me.

The sound of a truck driving by had us turning. One of the ranch hands was driving by, heading down the driveway to the bunk house and stable area.

"Oh my god."

I glanced down at Natalie. Over the course of two

seconds, her demeanor had changed entirely. Her muscles tightened and her breath caught.

"What's the matter?"

"That truck. I've seen it before."

Okay.

"Yesterday. I thought I saw...no." She shook her head and turned to go inside.

I cupped her biceps and spun her about. "What?"

"I'm pretty sure I saw that truck, that I saw Patrick just after the tire blow out."

I stared at her for a few seconds, took in the seriousness of her dark eyes, the confidence of her words. She sounded unsure, it seemed, not because it wasn't true, but because she didn't *want* it to be true. Glancing up, Ashe was frowning. She'd met Patrick before, a quick introduction the first day she was here and then again yesterday when we took the horses out. She knew what he looked like. Knew his name.

"I'll get Archer." Ashe went inside.

A minute later, he came back with Archer who held a bottle of beer in his hand. He was dressed in jeans and a flannel shirt, clearly off duty. He shook my hand and greeted Natalie. "Ashe said you wanted to share something."

Natalie nodded, wiped her hands on her jeans. "Yesterday, after the tire blew, a guy stopped to help. You met him."

Archer nodded. "John Feranski."

"Right. But another car passed soon after. Well, a truck." She glanced up at me. "Patrick's."

Archer gave no outward sign of surprise, definitely a nod to his experience as a sheriff. I was fucking stunned.

"You're sure?"

Natalie thought for a second. Nodded. "Yes. I know there are a million pickup trucks in Montana. I mean, each one of you men drives one. But his is pretty old and well, has those ridiculous truck nuts on the hitch and the red mud flaps."

"True," Archer added, looking toward the bunk house as if he could see Patrick's truck from here.

"Yesterday, I didn't really notice the truck, but I noticed Patrick driving. He caught my eye and surprised me since we were in the middle of nowhere. When he didn't stop, I figured I was wrong because any one of you would've. But then when I saw the truck go by just now, and him behind the wheel, I remembered the details."

Patrick had been up on the pass, saw the women's car tire blow out and hadn't stopped? It didn't seem like him. Hell, any Montanan stopped when someone was in trouble. It was a wild place and everyone watched out for each other, even strangers. The guy, Feranski, was an example. But why the fuck was Patrick up there in the first place? And right then?

"You don't think he put that tire spike in the road, do you?" Ashe asked, tipping his voice low.

What. The. Fuck?

Archer glanced in the open door. All was quiet within.

"I don't know, but it's worth looking into."

"Are you shitting me?" I ran my hand over the back of my neck. "You think Patrick wanted to hurt the women?"

Archer didn't respond, but instead said, "The tires on Kady's SUV are a year old. Full tread still. Cord and Riley wouldn't risk shitty tires on a vehicle Kady drives. And now that they have Cecily...they're protective as fuck."

Weren't we all?

"You mean it shouldn't have just blown," I added, trying to calm down and not storm off to the bunk house and beat the shit out of Patrick and ask questions later. "You're thinking Patrick sabotaged the women's SUV?"

Natalie glanced between us, wide-eyed. "Oh, my god," she whispered, her fingers over her lips. Lips that had been around my dick at five this morning. And that little fucker had wanted to hurt her? He was going down.

Archer shrugged. "Don't go all ape shit." He looked to me and held up his hand in the stop gesture. "But the hole in the tire wasn't small. Not like a nail or something. It was ripped."

"Fuck," Ashe murmured, running a hand over his face. He walked over to the railing, leaned forward and set his hands on it. Stared out into the distance. His cheeks were flushed and his stance was tense. Yeah, he wanted to go deliver some Montana justice but was holding back.

"We'll invite the hands up for dinner, see what happens," Archer said.

"If he wanted to hurt the women, do we want him in the house?" I asked. "He should be in jail."

"We have no proof," he countered. "Yet. Besides Natalie seeing him, or thinking she saw him, there's nothing tying him to the blown tire."

Ashe pushed off the railing and turned. "But—" he began.

"I believe you, Natalie," Archer said, cutting Ashe off. "Don't think otherwise. But we can't just confront him. It's not how this is done. I'll get Cricket to invite the men up for dinner. It's not unusual for her to do so. I'll make a few calls to the station. Let's keep this between the four of us for now. If Patrick really did this, then the most important thing is for all of us not to stare at him funny over a meal. Or have one of the other men beat the shit out of him. He has to think we have no clue."

"I'm a terrible actress," Natalie admitted.

She was rubbing her arms, so I pulled her back against me, wrapped my arms around her.

"Don't worry, your sisters are crazy enough to be a distraction." Archer smiled.

I angled my head so I could see Natalie's face and saw that his words made her smile, too.

"I'll take care of this, all right?" Archer added. "Don't worry. If Patrick did this, he's going down. One way or another."

Absolutely. And I doubted Archer would even get him in handcuffs. He'd have to deal with all the men inside—plus us here on the porch—first. There was a lot of land on Steele Ranch to hide a body.

$\mathcal{N}$ATALIE

PATRICK AND SHAMUS came to eat dinner, just as Archer had assumed. He'd told Cricket that she she shouldn't take no for an answer to her invite. Luring men with food wasn't all that hard to do. And by the look of Patrick—and Shamus—they were young college kids who could put a side of beef away.

Since there was so many of us, eighteen, we'd put platters of grilled hamburgers, pasta salad, chips and brownies out on the counter and everyone had helped themselves. Some had sat at the large dining room table, others on the couch to watch a baseball game as they ate. I'd sat at a stool at the kitchen counter, Sam at my side. If he got up, Ashe took his spot. It should have been smothering, not being allowed out of their sight, but today, I was just fine with that.

It had been easy to steer clear of Patrick because Cricket had pulled me into the kitchen to help with the dishes. It had been the first time I was glad to do them. Patrick was on one of the couches in the other room watching the ball game so it didn't seem like I was hiding. I did notice Archer remained nearby and kept an eye on him.

But Patrick was completely normal. He'd made small talk with everyone, but he was a little wary around chatting us ladies up too much. Having big, alpha males for boyfriends/husbands probably made him wary about getting too friendly. Since Riley and Jamison knew nothing about our conversation on the porch, they were talking batter stats with him.

But conversation turned to the flat tire incident. I could hear the men debating whether we'd hit a patch of ice or if there had been a nail. I glanced at Cricket, who was drying the platter I'd just handed her. My hands were deep in suds and hot water, but I grabbed an extra dish towel and wiped them off. "I want to hear this."

She quickly finished drying and put the platter on the counter. "Me, too. The dishes can wait."

There was no faking my curiosity, and I knew

Cricket would want any updates, too. I followed her into the other room, but as she went over to sit on the arm of the couch by Archer, I went the other way and toward Ashe. He patted his lap and I sat down. I had no intention of getting it on like Penny and Boone had earlier, but sitting with Ashe was far from the same thing.

Cecily had been fussy and so Kady had taken her upstairs about a half hour ago to nurse. Since they hadn't returned, I had to assume they were both taking a nap. Although, Cord was missing, so perhaps they were getting busy in some quiet corner of this big house.

"That guardrail and steep edge were too damned close," Boone said, slowly shaking his head.

"Natalie, you're teaching all of us winter driving skills come first snowfall," Archer added, giving me a small nod.

Ashe leaned forward and kissed my temple as the others agreed.

"The mechanic can easily replace the tire and fix the back panel, but he'll also check for any other damage," Riley said. "Fortunately, Kady's still on maternity leave from school, so we can drive her wherever she needs to go."

"You're going to have to let her go off by herself again sometime soon," Cricket advised.

Riley shook his head. "Fuck, no. Look what happened when we did that."

The other men murmured their agreement.

I shook my head at their caveman antics.

"I'm going to go to the bathroom," I murmured to Ashe as I pushed off his lap. He made to stand. "Oh no. You can drive me around if that makes you feel better, but I can pee all by myself."

I flicked my gaze to the other couch where Patrick still sat. He hadn't joined in the conversation about the blown tire, but he hadn't been there. Or if he had, he wasn't saying. He was being supervised by more than a handful of men. I was safe.

Instead of returning to the great room—I wasn't a big fan of baseball—I returned to the kitchen through the entry off the hallway. I picked up the platter Cricket had dried to put it away. Squatting down, I opened one of the low cabinets.

"You're pretty good at driving."

I glanced up, saw Patrick looming over me. He was handsome, but his eyes held...something. My heart skipped a beat, but I quickly put the platter away, then stood. He didn't move back. He smelled like he'd had one too many beers.

"Thanks." I gave him a quick fake smile. "It was pretty scary. And we were lucky."

He slowly shook his head. "Lucky? Yeah, you and

your sisters are really lucky." He paused and I held my breath. "I mean, look at this place."

He gestured with his hand in a big circle.

"The house is beautiful," I agreed. I tried to skirt around him, but he stepped in my way.

"What do you want, Patrick?" I asked, trying to stay as calm as possible.

He didn't look calm now. He looked a little drunk, a little pissed.

"Yes, Patrick, what do you want?" Sam said. Ashe stood beside him.

Patrick turned at the sound of his voice and I quickly darted around him and to Sam's side. He was leaning against the peninsula, arms crossed. He tucked me into his side as I approached. I was thankful he was there to rescue me...and that I hadn't had to torque Patrick's fingers like I had Alan's.

"What do I want?" He shook his head, ran his hands over the top of his head as if he had a migraine, messing up his blond hair. When he looked our way again, his eyes were wild. "I want what's rightfully mine."

"What's rightfully yours?" Archer asked, coming into the room from the hallway as I had. His hands were at his sides, palms out.

Riley, Lee and Boone appeared at the far side of the counter, looking into the kitchen. Sutton came and stood beside me. There was no way out of the kitchen. The plan to be low key, to let Archer take care of it, appeared to be short lived. For some reason, Patrick was cracking now. Perhaps it was the beer or the talk of the accident. Or maybe he just snapped.

"Everything," Patrick shouted.

I startled at his sudden intensity.

"You seem upset," Archer said. His tone was slow. Even. While he wasn't wearing his uniform, he was all sheriff. "Why don't you tell us what you mean?"

Patrick shook his head, glanced at the floor, then back at Archer.

"This house, the land, the money is mine. Mine!"

Sam's hand flexed around my waist.

"Why is it yours?" Archer prodded.

"Because Aiden Steele's my father, too!"

Holy shit. Patrick was my half-brother? Out of the six of us, he'd be the youngest, even younger than Penny by a few years. He had to be twenty or so. Maybe twenty-one.

"There was no mention of you in the will," Riley said. Everyone turned to look at him.

Patrick's eyes narrowed and his cheeks reddened. "Yes, I'm fucking aware of that. Why do you think *they* have all the money and I don't?" He pointed at me as if I represented all the Steele sisters.

"Why aren't you mentioned in the will, Patrick?" Archer asked.

He spun about, faced Archer. "Because he told me I was a worthless sack of shit." I gasped and his feral eyes looked to me. "That's right, daddy dearest didn't like me."

"Why is that?" Archer asked. He was prodding Patrick, getting him to talk, but he was also directing the conversation, getting him to go where he wanted. I had no idea where that was, but it seemed he had an idea. It was as if he knew something, something big and was trying to get Patrick to admit to it. Perhaps my seeing him right after the tire blew was the puzzle piece Archer had been looking for.

"He never saw me. Never paid me any attention. Hell, I got the job here just to be close to him, but he didn't even recognize me." He laughed. "I'm his son and he didn't recognize me! So I killed that cow. *That* got his attention."

"You broke open the fence and let the stud horse in with the mares in the paddock," Sutton added from beside me.

"That was a good one, too, right? If they're going to fuck, why keep them apart?"

A sound of disgust came from Sutton's throat, but he said nothing. Didn't even move. He was in charge of the horses here, but I wasn't familiar with what that entailed. And I had no idea why getting a stud horse in with a bunch of mares was bad, but it sounded like it was.

"You sabotaged shit to what, get Aiden's attention?" Jamison asked.

"He figured out it was me and he confronted me. I told him the truth, that I was his son. That he'd fucked my mother and left her to slave over two jobs just to support us. That he'd known she was pregnant and abandoned us both. And then...then, he said a man who stoops to killing and putting horses in danger isn't worth being his son."

Patrick was insane. He'd killed a cow to get his dad's attention.

"I've known Aiden a long time," Jamison said. "He was a grumpy fucker, but he would never have left a woman pregnant and alone. He might not have married her, but he'd have done right by her."

"My mother said—"

"Maybe your mother's a liar," Archer snapped.

That only enraged Patrick even more. Had it been intentional?

"Fuck you! And Aiden Steele can just rot in his grave."

"A grave you put him in. Right?"

The room was dead silent because of Archer's words. Only Patrick's riled breathing could be heard.

Patrick killed my father? *Our* father? Had Archer known? No, but he was figuring it out pretty darn fast.

Patrick grinned then. Widely. Wickedly. Oh shit. He had killed Aiden Steele.

"Let's just say it wasn't a heart attack that knocked him off the horse."

"Oh fuck," Sam murmured. He pushed me back behind him now that we knew Patrick wasn't just a ranch hand. He was a murderer.

14

*N*ATALIE

"You killed him because you hated him," Archer continued. "And you killed him because you wanted everything he had. If he wasn't going to give you love, you'd take everything else, right?"

"Exactly. He didn't want anything to do with me. He wouldn't tell anyone I was his son."

"So you took what he wouldn't give you."

Patrick nodded. "That's right. I earned it! It's mine."

"But then you found out it wasn't just you who inherited the land, but five sisters."

Patrick spun about, put his hands on the counter.

Everyone stared at his back, watched, waited. I didn't even think anyone was breathing.

"Five sisters who you didn't even know existed. If you had, you wouldn't have killed him, right? I mean, why would you want to share the inheritance with five women?"

Archer talked as if we were in an interrogation room, not a kitchen.

"They ruined everything. Everything!" Patrick spun about and stepped toward me, eyes narrowed, nostrils flaring. There was no way he'd get to me through Ashe, Sam and Sutton, but I still flinched back. He was beyond mad, he was eaten up by it. Crazed.

"Aiden Steele never told me about you. He never put you in his will," Riley added. He was the lawyer and knew things none of us did. "Which means, you get nothing."

"Not unless all of the sisters are dead," Archer continued.

"DNA would prove I was his son. That it was all mine. I'd get it all!"

"So you tossed spikes onto the road. What did you do, wait for them to come up the road? I mean, you couldn't have just put them out at any time. You didn't want to kill the wrong people."

Patrick rubbed his hands together. "Binoculars. That SUV's like an aircraft carrier. Can't miss it on that straightaway."

"But you missed a spike when you stopped to pick them up after the tire blew."

"And they didn't go over the guardrail on the bend."

"That wasn't the first time you tried to harm one of the women, is it?" Archer asked.

Penny wheedled her way in beside Jamison and he tucked her into his side. Close. Cricket settled in next to Lee as Sarah stood with Wilder and King behind the others. While they didn't have a front row seat, they couldn't miss what was going on.

Patrick's eyes lit up and he started to talk. It was as if he had to tell us everything, that he'd held these secrets in for so long, that he seemed *proud* of his activities.

"I didn't have to do a thing for Kady. Hell, she had a fucking hit man after her. Unfortunately, he wasn't successful in his task. Penny was *almost* a success. That guy at the bar made contact and—"

"He was going to take her out the back door of the Silky Spur and rape her," Jamison growled. Penny turned her face into his chest, hugged him.

Patrick shrugged. "Yeah, and you thought our lack of escort to the restroom was because we lacked gentlemanly traits." He laughed. God, it gave me chills. "More like I wanted her to suffer. Sarah though, well, no one knew she even existed. It was pretty hard to try and kill someone who was a secret. Then she was married to King and Wilder and impossible to get to."

Jamison's jaw clenched and he tugged Penny even closer. She was crying now, silently, but tears streamed down her cheeks.

"And Cricket?" Archer asked, his voice deep, barely hanging on by a thread now that he asked after his woman.

"It wasn't too hard to get that idiot to camp out in her apartment."

I was amazed by Archer's restraint, that he didn't kill him but instead only punched Patrick in the face. Blood spurted from his nose as the impact rocked him back, slamming into the edge of the counter. It seemed Archer had heard enough. He pulled his cell phone from his shirt pocket, tossed it to Sutton who caught it easily.

When I glanced at it, I saw Archer had been recording the whole thing.

Archer tugged Patrick's hand behind his back, pressed his head down into the counter as he kicked his feet apart and frisked him.

"Get me the cuffs out of my truck," Archer snapped, keeping his attention squarely on Patrick. His breathing was ragged, his cheeks flushed. I heard heavy footfall behind us, the front door open.

"Patrick Monaghan, you're under arrest. You have the right to remain silent, you so much as fucking blink, the—"

As Archer read him his rights—with a little extra—

I turned my face into Sam's chest. He was warm and strong, his scent familiar and my mind recognized it as safety. He was my anchor and so was Ashe. He led me out of the kitchen and into the great room. Tipping up my chin, he made me look at him. "Are you all right?"

I licked my lips. "Stunned."

King returned with the handcuffs and walked past us into the kitchen.

"I called 9-1-1 a few minutes ago," Cord said, his arm around Kady who held Cecily. "I'm sure someone else has, too. They'll be here in a few."

"We missed most of it," Kady added, looking disappointed.

I stared at her for a second, stunned, then I burst out laughing.

"Only you, Kady. Only you."

I pulled her in for a hug, careful of Cecily.

The kitchen was full with most of the men ensuring Patrick didn't get away. It was one thing to be the nut job who killed Aiden Steele, but it was another entirely to want to kill their women. *That* crossed the line for them, I was sure, and no doubt considered killing Patrick because of it justifiable homicide.

Sarah, Penny and Cricket joined us so we stood in a tight circle.

"This is insane," Sarah said, glancing toward the kitchen. "We have a half-brother who's obviously criminally insane who killed our father and tried to kill all of us for the money. If he'd just come forward, said he was one of Aiden Steele's kids, too, I'd have shared it with him."

"Me, too," Cricket added.

Kady, Penny and I nodded.

Fussing came from the other side of the room and Penny broke off to go get Locke from where he'd been sleeping in his car seat. He'd slept through everything. She returned with him over her shoulder. He stared at us wide-eyed, yet still sleepy, content to be in his mother's arms.

"That man, at the bar that night, I'd thought he was just a handsy jerk," Penny recounted. I didn't know the story, but it could have been bad. "But after what Patrick said, he'd sent him to hurt me." She shivered and Sarah wrapped her arms around her. "Patrick was there, in the bar, too. We'd even driven together, had drinks. Danced. God, if Jamison and Boone hadn't showed up."

"You're fine. We're all fine," Cricket reassured. "We can't think about all of that or we'll never sleep at night. Let's think about...Natalie!"

I frowned at Cricket's surprisingly Kady-like outburst. "Me?"

All four of my sisters eyed me. Cord, Sam and Ashe, too.

"Yes, you. This probably wasn't good to help the cause for you sticking around, but you've got to stay here in Barlow. I mean, we're sisters and we've *literally* survived a lot together."

It was true. We had. In a matter of days, they were the crazy family I'd heard about—minus the crazy half-brother—and never knew I'd missed.

"I'm staying," I replied immediately.

The women pounced on me, pulling me into a group hug that was happy laughing and shedding some tears. Locke fussed. "But you're not the top reason why I'm staying. Sorry," I said through the big hug. I pulled back and turned to face Ashe and Sam.

"You two are the reason why I want to stay." I looked at them, met their eyes. Held. They'd looked at me just like this in the hallway of the restaurant in Boston. Eagerness, hope. Intense interest. But there was something more now, too. Love.

"If the offer still stands, I want to—"

Ashe had me in his arms, his lips on mine before I could finish. I vaguely heard more whoops and excitement, but the kiss was just too good.

And when Ashe was done, or maybe before he was, Sam tugged me into his arms and his lips were on mine next.

"Get a room," Cord said, his tone joking.

Sam pulled back and smiled down at me.

God, I wanted them.

"I know I said I wouldn't fuck you with others

around, but, well...I need you." I took Ashe's hand, then Sam's. "Now."

Sam looked around.

"Not the coffee table!" Cricket called.

"The door in the office has seen a lot of action. It's a little hard against your back though," Penny advised.

"The laundry room works pretty well," Kady added.

God, was there anywhere in the house someone hadn't had sex?

"Upstairs," Ashe said, tugging me toward the hallway. "A coffee table's fine, so is a door. Never tried a washing machine, but I do like a bed."

"Have fun!" Sarah called out.

I glanced at Sam, whose gaze was so hot I was surprised it didn't singe off my clothes. "Desperate times call for desperate pleasures."

ASHE

I WANTED to go in and beat the shit out of Patrick, but the line was long. After everyone else had their turn, I doubted there would be much left. With over ten witnesses of him confessing to not only killing Aiden

Steele, but to attempted murder on all five women and two babies and...

I gritted my teeth, took a breath as I pulled Natalie up the stairs. Everyone was fine. Patrick was being taken care of. The other women had their men nearby. Sam and I had Natalie and we were never letting her go. Not now that she said she was staying.

God, those words. I'd have gone to Boston for her. Belize, Bangkok, wherever. But the fact that she was staying right here in Barlow because of us?

Best fucking feeling ever. There was still much to talk about. Her job, where to live, but we'd work it out. What mattered was that we'd be together.

I had so much love, so much need for her that I was out of my mind. It wasn't just my dick that was leading the way this time. So was my heart.

I had a feeling he wasn't getting out of jail for a long, long time. That would help me sleep at night. And having Natalie in my arms.

I'd never been on the second floor before, but I peeked in the first door we passed and saw that it was definitely Cricket's. Women's clothing over the back of the chair by the window. Although, it could have been one of the guys' rooms. Either way, I wasn't fucking Natalie in there. I went further down the hall, past a bathroom and to a much smaller bedroom. Tucked beneath the eaves at the back of the house, the bed was made, the room neat and it appeared unused.

Perfect.

I tugged Natalie in and Sam shut the door behind us.

We were too far away to hear anything from the front of the house—thank fuck. That also meant no one downstairs would hear Natalie cry out as we made her come. Perfect.

Natalie looked at me with such need that it made me suck in a breath. And when she launched herself at me, her arms going around my neck, her legs around my waist, I oomphed. But just for a second because her lips were on mine and her tongue was in my mouth. My dick pressed against my jeans, eager to get to her. Fuck, she was so hot and frantic.

It was heaven, fucking heaven to have her so eager. I was the one who pulled back. "Easy, tiger," I said, grinning. "Don't forget about Sam."

She looked over her shoulder at Sam, reached one arm out toward him, beckoning him to join us.

"I want this to be quick," she said, her breathing ragged. Sam took a step closer and she dropped her hands between us to my belt, undoing the buckle. *Shit.* "I need you. I need your cocks in me. Now."

I turned and carried her to the bed, laid her down and followed so I hovered over her. I let her open my pants, get my dick in her tiny grip. "This isn't going to be fast, sweetheart. Not this time."

"You want both of us?" Sam asked, coming to stand at the end of the bed, his hands on the brass footboard.

Natalie looked up at him, bit her lip. "Yes."

"Together?" I added.

I let that question sink in, let her take a minute to understand what we were asking. We'd played with her ass, got her used to us being there, but taking both our dicks at the same time was different. So much more.

"Yes, together. Just like you promised."

Lifting up, I reached down, took off her boots, let them drop to the floor. Her socks followed. Then I worked her jeans down her hips, taking her panties with them. I saw a hint of yellow satin, but didn't take the time to peek. Her sexy panties were so fucking hot, but her, naked, was so much better.

She lifted her hips, helped me and then she was bare from the waist down. I dropped to my knees at the side of the bed, hooked the back of her knees and pulled her toward me. I couldn't miss how wet she was and my mouth watered to get that sticky sweetness on my tongue.

As I ate her out, I looked up her body, watched as Sam went to the opposite side of the bed, reached and tugged the hem of her shirt up. She raised her arms for him to pull it off. He took hold of her wrists, captured them so they were straight over her head. Captured.

Her breasts were covered in a pretty bra of yellow

satin. With his free hand, Sam tugged down the cups, one after the other so her breasts were exposed, the nipples taut and pointing right at the ceiling. Sam leaned forward, took one in his mouth.

I realized then I was barely licking her, the sight of Sam holding our girl down and playing with her was incredible to see. But she wiggled and whimpered and I wanted to get her off before we got in her.

"I want to suck you," Natalie breathed.

Sam popped up, looked down at her. He was able to open his jeans and pull out his dick without releasing her hands. "You want to blow me while Ashe fucks you with his tongue?"

"Yes, please. I want to taste you. Feel how big you are against my tongue, deep in my throat."

Sam growled as his dick pulsed in his fist.

Leaning forward, he settled one hand on the mattress by her side so his dick hovered right over her mouth. Her tongue flicked out, licked the tip.

"Fuck, sweetheart. You can have a taste, but I'm coming deep in your ass."

Natalie opened her mouth wide and I watched as Sam's dick disappeared an inch at a time.

He lifted his head, looked at me. Fuck, I knew what her mouth felt like around my dick, that sweet suction. "Hurry, man."

If he wanted to fill her ass with his cum instead of her mouth, I had to hurry, just like he said.

So I stopped watching and got to work. I slipped two fingers into her pussy, found her g-spot as I focused my tongue on the left side of her clit, just where I knew to get her off. It was time to stop teasing and push her to the edge and over.

And that happened fast. Thank fuck since I was going to blow.

Sam slipped from her lips, his dick shiny just before she came. With her wrists still captive in his, she could barely move. Her back curved as she came, clenching and milking my fingers, eager for more. She dripped all over them, her body soft and swollen, slick and ready for my dick.

As she recovered, I heard the drawer open and Sam's words, "Of course this house has lube in every room."

Sam had gone to find some lube, knowing while her pussy was dripping, she needed some help to get his dick in that ass. We wouldn't have her hurting.

"Ready to take both of us?" I asked her. I loomed over her once again, took in her sated look, the soft smile.

"Mmm," she replied.

"Natalie," I said.

Her eyes flickered open.

"I love you. You're what brings us together as a family. I'm glad you've decided to stay with us, but know this, we'd have gone with you. Wherever you are is where I want to be. As long as we're together."

Tears filled her eyes as she smiled. She lifted up on an elbow, hooked her hand about my neck and kissed me.

"Is that what I taste like?" She licked my lips once, then again.

"Sweet like honey? Fuck yes."

"I have no idea what I'm going to do for a job, but right about now, I don't care. I have money saved and well, Aiden Steele gave me the opportunity to figure it out. And, he brought me both of you. Without him, I'd never be here with you. I'd never have found love. It's time. I'm ready. I choose both of you. Now fuck me."

15

NATALIE

THEY MIGHT BE the dominant ones, but in that moment, I was in control. They'd had me all but pinned to the bed; Sam's hands on my wrists, his cock deep in my mouth and Ashe's head between my thighs. Not that I'd had any interest in moving. But now, I got them moving.

And fast.

Sam dropped the bottle of lube on the bed so he could undress.

Ashe stood and stripped off his clothes so his dick stood out, long, thick and proud. A bead of pre-cum oozed from the slit and I leaned forward to lick it up.

He stopped me with a hand. "Oh no. Every drop is going in that pussy."

Putting a knee on the bed, he moved to the middle and settled, gripping me at the waist and lifting me up so he could straighten his legs.

I straddled him, his cock nestled between us. My bra was uncomfortable so I reached back, undid the clasp and shrugged it off.

"Better?" he asked, cupping my breasts in his big hands.

I nodded, moaned as he tugged on my sensitive nipples. He had to feel how much I liked it since I just dripped all over him.

"Up you go. Let's get your crammed full, sweetheart."

I went up on my knees as his hands slid to my waist, helping me settle on him, then lower, taking him all the way to the root.

We both groaned. He was big, so big and deep. I loved it this way because I could take so much of him. I leaned down, kissed him, my breasts pressing into his chest.

"Good girl," Sam said. "Stay right like that."

I felt the bed dip as he moved behind me. Cool, slick fingers pressed against my back entrance, then slipped inside. Two at once.

I gasped into the kiss. It didn't hurt, quite the opposite, but it was...weird. The feeling was intense, especially with Ashe already in me. He started to lift and lower me, which only worked Sam's slick fingers into me deeper. He retreated, added more lube, slid deep. Stretching me, preparing me.

"That's it, open up. Yes. Fuck, Natalie. It's time."

Sam's fingers slid from me and I heard the slick sound of more lube.

Ashe cupped my chin. "Look at me. I want to see your face when you take us both for the first time."

My eyes widened as I felt the broad head of Sam's cock nudging me, then pressing. He was insistent, but careful. I focused on breathing, on relaxing, but it was hard—and so was Sam.

I clenched Ashe's shoulders, but held his gaze. Sweat dotted his brow, obviously straining to keep himself still.

"Ah!" I cried when Sam popped inside.

"Shit, so tight, sweetheart."

Carefully, he pushed in, then back, fucking me slowly, carefully. Deeper and deeper until his hips pressed against my bottom.

My eyes were wide as I stared at Ashe, saw the way his mouth turned up.

"Well? How is it being fucked by your two men?"

"You aren't fucking me yet," I countered.

Sam pulled back and his cock hit every nerve ending within me.

"Oh god," I moaned.

As he slid back in, Ashe pulled his hips back. A back and forth motion, one in, the other out. Fucking me.

"That's it. Take us both. You can't do anything but feel. Let your men take care of you. Love you. Make you feel so good," Sam crooned.

Sounds of our ragged breathing filled the room. Slick sounds of fucking, too. This was it, the most amazing thing. Sex made the bonds of love strong, but this, with both of them, was the most intense thing I'd ever felt.

Just like Sam said, I couldn't do anything but feel. And come.

The pleasure was too intense, my need for them too great. That first orgasm hadn't cooled my ardor, only made me even greedier. And now I took.

Both men. Both cocks. All the pleasure they could give.

I came, clenching down on both of them. My back arched, my bottom pushing back and taking them both deeper. More.

I cried out, groaned, clenched. Just gave over to the amazing bliss.

I was lost. Loved. Held. Well and truly fucked.

Sam thrust deep one last time, shouted my name as he came. I could feel the heat of him as he filled me. Ashe was seconds later, his grip on my hips tightening and his cum flooding me, dripping out.

We were a sweaty, sticky mess and I couldn't have been happier.

Carefully, Sam pulled out and went into the en suite bathroom. Ashe rolled us to the side, his cock slipping free. Cum dripped from me, a blatant and virile sign that I was truly theirs.

Sam came back with a wet cloth and they each took a thigh, parted me so he could clean me up. It was so intimate, this care.

Then he cleaned himself and tossed the washcloth on the floor.

Sliding into bed with us, he grabbed the sheet, tugged it up.

"Welcome home, sweetheart." Sam leaned over, kissed me, stroked my arm with his knuckles. Ashe kissed along my shoulder, his hand on my belly as if neither of them could stop touching me.

I closed my eyes, felt loved.

We were in a guest bedroom at Steele Ranch. Definitely not our home. But I knew what he meant. I was home. With Sam and Ashe. Between them. Right where I wanted to be.

NOTE FROM VANESSA

Yes, it's the end of the Steele Ranch saga.

But guess what? I've got some bonus content for you—stop by Steele Ranch three years later and see what everyone's up to. So sign up for my mailing list. There's special bonus content for each Steele Ranch book, just for my subscribers. Signing up will let you hear about my next release as soon as it is out, too (and you get a free book...wow!)

As always...thanks for loving my books and the wild ride!

WANT MORE?

A new Vanessa Vale series! Kick off the Small Town Romance series with Montana Fire. Check out this sneak peek!

MONTANA FIRE - CHAPTER ONE

"I'm not sure which one I want. I didn't realize there were so many choices!"

The woman wasn't on the hunt for a new car or juice boxes at the grocery store. Nope. She wanted a dildo. I called her type a Waffler. Someone who contemplated all options before even attempting to make a choice. Because of Miss Waffler, I had ten different dildo options spread out across the counter. Glass, silicone, jelly and battery powered. She needed help.

That's where I came in. My name is Jane West and I run Goldilocks, the adult store in Bozeman, Montana, my mother-in-law had opened back in the seventies. Story goes she named it after the fairytale character when a mother bear and her two cubs strolled down Willson right in front of the store the week before it opened. She called it fate. Or it could have been because her name is Goldie, so it made sense. I started working for her when my husband died, a temporary arrangement that helped her out. Three years later, things had turned long-term temporary.

The store was tasteful considering the offerings. The walls were a fresh white with shelves and displays just like you'd find at the typical department store. Then tasteful made way for tacky. Gold toned industrial carpet like you'd see in Vegas, a photo of a naked woman sprawled artfully across a bearskin rug hung over the counter. A sixties chandelier graced the meager entry. Goldie had to put her unique stamp on things somehow.

It wasn't a big store, just one room with a storage area and bathroom in back. Whatever she didn't have in stock—although you'd be amazed at the selection Goldie offered in such a small space—we ordered in. Montanans were patient shoppers. With few options store-wise in Bozeman, most people ordered everything but the basics from the Internet. There's one Walmart, one Target, one Old Navy. Only one of everything. In a big city, if you drove two miles you came across a repeat store. Urban sprawl at its finest. Not here, although there were two sets of Golden Arches. One in town and one off the highway for the tourists who needed a Big Mac on the way to Yellowstone. The anchor store of the town's only mall was a chain bookstore. No Nordstrom or Bass Pro Shop out here. You shopped local or you went home to your computer.

In the case of the woman in front of me, I wished she'd just go home.

Don't get me wrong, I liked helping people and I was comfortable talking sex toys with anyone. But this time was definitely different. Big time.

Behind Miss Waffler stood a fireman. A *really* attractive, tall, well-muscled one wearing a Bozeman Fire T-shirt and navy pants. Can you say hot? A *hot* man in uniform? Yup, it was a cliché, but this one was dead-on accurate. God, he was literally heart stopping gorgeous. He'd made mine skip a beat. I felt all tingly and hot all over.

He'd come in while I was comparing the various dildo models before I went into the perks of having rotation for best female stimulation, and when I looked up...and up and he was there, I practically swallowed my tongue. I'd certainly lost my train of thought. I had no idea God made men like him. Magazines, maybe. Real life? *My* real life? Wow.

"Can you explain the features of each one again?" Miss Waffler had her fingers on the edge of the glass counter as if she were afraid to touch them. Petite, she was slim to the point of anorexic. Her rough voice said smoker, at least a pack a day. Her skin was weathered, either from cigarettes or the Montana weather, and wrinkles had taken over her face. She'd be pretty if she ate something and kicked the nicotine habit.

I gave her my best fake smile. "Sure."

I darted a glance at the fireman over the woman's shoulder. Sandy hair trimmed military short, blue eyes, strong features. Thirties. A great smile. He seemed perfectly content to wait his turn. If the humorous glint in his eye and the way he bit his lip— most likely to keep from smiling—was any indication, he was clearly enjoying himself. And learning something about dildos. Maybe he wanted some options for his girlfriend. He had to have some woman warming his bed. A radio squawked on his belt and he turned it down. Obviously, my lesson on sexual aids was more important than a five-alarm fire.

Miss Waffler was completely oblivious of, and unaffected by, the fireman. I now knew why she wanted a dildo.

I picked up a bright blue model. "This one is battery powered and vibrates. Ten settings. Good for clitoral stimulation." I put it down and picked up another. I was used to talking sex toys with people. Some guys, too, but I was dying of embarrassment having said *clitoral stimulation* in front of *him*. I just imagined this hot fireman stimulating my clit. I squirmed, cleared my throat and continued. "This one is glass. No batteries, so it's meant for penetration. The best thing about it is you can put it in the freezer or warm it and it provides a varied experience."

The woman made some *ah* sounds as I gave the details. I went through all the possibilities with her one at a time. I got to the tenth and final model. "This one is obviously realistic. It's actually molded from the erect penis of a porn star. It's made of silicone and has suction cups on the base."

Fireman peered over the woman's shoulder as I suction cupped the dildo to the glass counter. *Thwap.* He didn't seem too stunned by the size. Did that mean he was that big, too?

"You can...um, attach it to a piece of furniture if you want to keep your hands free."

Both fireman and Miss Waffler nodded their heads as if they could picture what I was talking about.

"I'll take that one," she said as she pointed to number ten. The eight-inch Whopper Dong.

"Good choice."

I rang up Miss Waffler's purchase and she happily went off to take care of business.

And there he was. Mr. Fireman. And me. And dildo display made three. Fortunately, he stood in front of the counter and I wasn't able to look down and see if his Whopper Dong fit inside his uniform pants. Oh god, I was going straight to hell. He saved people's lives and I was thinking about his—

"Um...thanks for waiting." I tucked my curly hair behind an ear.

"Sure. You learn something new every day." He smiled. Not just with his mouth, but with his eyes. Very blue eyes. I saw interest there. Heat, too.

Right there, in the middle of my mother-in-law's sex store, dildos and all, was the spring thaw in my libido. It had long since gone as cold as Montana in January. Who could have blamed it with all of my dead husband's shenanigans? But right then, I felt my heart rate go up, and my palms sweating from nerves. The fireman didn't seem the least bit fazed by my little sex toy talk. I, on the other hand, was having a hot flash like a menopausal woman just looking at him. I needed to be hosed down. Speaking of hoses—

"I'm Jane. What can I help you with today?" *Hi, I'm Jane. I'm thirty-three. I like hiking in the mountains, cross-country skiing, I'm a Scorpio, and I want to rip that uniform off your hot body and slide down your pole.* I wiped my sweaty palms on my shorts.

He laughed and held out his hand. His grip was firm, his skin warm and a little rough. "Ty. Thanks, but no toys for me." A pager beeped. He looked at it on his belt briefly and ignored it.

"Don't you need to answer that? A fire or something?" I asked, pointing to his waist.

"Cat up a tree," he joked, the corner of his full lips tipping up.

I laughed, and heard my nerves in it. I took a deep breath to try and calm my racing heart. It didn't work. All it did was make me discover how good he smelled. It wasn't heavy cologne. Soap maybe. I didn't really care if it was deodorant. He smelled fabulous.

"Actually, it was for Station Two. I'm here for your fire safety inspection." He placed papers on the counter. Had he been holding them all this time? I hadn't noticed.

"Oh, um...inspect away."

Inspect away?

He grinned at me as I blushed, ready to slink behind the counter and die of embarrassment. Fortunately, he switched topics. For the next fifteen minutes, we went over fire inspection paperwork with the attraction I felt for him an elephant in the room the shape of a dildo.

***

The next morning, I was out bright and early. If you lived in Montana, you got out and enjoyed good weather while the getting was good. Even in July. Especially in July. The days were long, the sky was big and there was a lot to do before it got cold. I didn't mean November like the real world. This was

Bozeman. Summer was over the day after Labor Day. It had even been known to snow in July. With that small window for wearing shorts and flip-flops and the threat of white flakes at any time, I was out and about by seven on a Saturday. I got more done before nine in the morning than the military. Not because I really wanted to, but because I had kids.

My boys, Zach and Bobby, were raring to go. Since it was Saturday morning, that meant garage sales. To kids, garage sales were serious business. Toys to be had, books to find. Even free stuff to rake in. As a grown up, I loved buying things I didn't know I needed. Last week, I bought a shoe rack for my closet and a toaster for the pop-up camper. For two dollars, I could have some toast while camping in the wilderness.

We were in the car, Kids Bop bounced out from the CD player. I had the hot garage sales circled in the classifieds, the *Bozeman Chronicle* open on the passenger seat next to me, ready to guide us to our treasures. The morning's first stop was a volunteer fire department's pancake breakfast. Bargain shopping could wait. With a pancake breakfast, I didn't have to cook—at seven in the morning, who wanted to?—the kids could stuff their faces, and I could get coffee. *Coffee.*

I realized the boys were yakking at me, so I turned down a sugary version of *Dynamite* to listen.

"He's so cool, Mom. He's a fireman and he was a

soldier and he said we could play in his yard. He's at least seven feet tall. His snow blower is bigger than ours. His truck is silver and it has four doors," Zach said from his booster in the back.

"He gave me a high five after I ridden my bike down the sidewalk. His name is Mr. Strickland," Bobby added. I peeked in the rearview mirror and saw him nod his head, super serious.

The man I'd heard about ever since the boys woke me up was Mr. Strickland, the new neighbor. Mr. Strickland did this, Mr. Strickland did that. The boys' new super hero had bought the house two doors down and just moved in. I hadn't met him yet, but the kids obviously had. In my coffee deprived mind, I pictured a fifty-something man with half a head of graying hair, a slight paunch—he was a fireman, so it couldn't be too big—and by Zach's description, taller than a basketball player. Great. He'd come in real handy when another ball got stuck up in the gutter.

"The Colonel likes him a lot," Zach said.

Well, that settled it. If the Colonel gave his approval, the man had to be all right, regardless of gargantuan size. The Colonel's real name is William Reinhoff, but everyone who knew him, which was the entire town, called him Colonel. He'd earned the title while fighting in Vietnam and it stuck. Gruff and ornery on the outside with a campfire toasted marshmallow center, he was one of my favorite people.

The Colonel's house was wedged between Mr. Strickland's and mine. He was next-door neighbor, pseudo father, close friend, occasional babysitter, and my mother's long-distance boyfriend. The kids had obviously met Mr. Strickland with the Colonel while I was at work yesterday and the man had made a serious impression. No way would the Colonel let the kids call the man by his first name. He was entirely too old school for that.

I pulled into the packed dirt parking lot of the fire department, parked, and turned to the kids. They sat in their boosters with the dollar bills I'd given each of them to spend on garage sale paraphernalia clenched in their fists. At seven, Zach was string bean skinny with knobby knees and dimples. Blond hair and light eyes had him looking like me. No one was sure where Bobby got his black hair and dark eyes as they surely hadn't come from either me or his father. Some people said he might be the Fed Ex man's kid, but I didn't see much humor in that. My husband had been the cheater, not me.

"Take only what you can eat, good manners, and put your dollar bill in your pocket so you don't lose it," I reminded them.

The kids nodded their heads with excitement. Garage sales and pancakes. Could life get any better?

The sun felt warm on my face. It had just popped up over the mountains, even though it had been light for almost two hours. "Leave your sweatshirts in the car. It'll be warm when we come out." I stripped off my fleece jacket and tossed it onto the front seat. It might have been summer, but it still dropped into the forties overnight.

The breakfast was in the fire department's bay. One big space, concrete floor and walls made of gray sheet metal siding. Two fire trucks were parked out in front with volunteer firemen watching kids swarm over the equipment. My two looked longingly at the apparatus but knew they could explore only once they'd eaten. Inside, it smelled like bacon and coffee. Two of my favorite things. I collected paper plates and plastic utensils and got in the buffet line for food.

"There's Jack from school," Zach said as he tugged on my arm and pointed. I waved to Jack and his parents who were already digging into their pancakes at one of the long tables. Everywhere you went in Bozeman, you ran into someone you knew. It was impossible to avoid it. Even a seven-year-old like Zach felt popular. It was nice sometimes, the sense of community, but once I'd ducked around an aisle at the grocery store to avoid someone so I didn't have to talk to them. Who hasn't? That time it had been my dental hygienist, and I hadn't been overly interested in being interrogated about my flossing practice.

Since I ran Goldilocks, the only adult store nearby —you had to go all the way to Billings otherwise—I had a lot of customers. Local customers. It was hard sometimes to make small talk with someone at the deli counter when you really only knew them from the time they came to the store to purchase nipple clamps for the little wife. Thus, the ducking around in stores. I held a lot of confidences, kept a lot of secrets, and over the years, the general population trusted me with them.

We approached the first breakfast offering. At the word 'eggs', the boys stuck out their plates. I watched them load up and move on to hash browns, which they skipped over with a polite, "No, thank you." I gave myself an imaginary pat on the back for their good manners. They could squawk like roosters at each other but were almost always polite to strangers who offered food.

"Mom! There's Mr. Strickland!" Zach practically yelled.

"Hi, Mr. Strickland!" Bobby chimed.

I searched for Mr. Strickland over the crowd of tables, down the length of the food, looking for the Mr. Strickland of my imagination. Where was the fifty-something man? The paunch? Zach held out his plate for pancakes.

"Hey, Champ!" the pancake man said to Zach.

My heart jumped into my throat and I broke out in an adrenaline-induced sweat.

"Holy crap," I said.

Pancake man was not fifty. Not even forty. He most definitely didn't have a pot belly. Only an incredibly flat one under a navy fire department T-shirt. Solid. Hot. Zach had certainly exaggerated Mr. Strickland's height. He was tall. I had to tilt my head up a bit to look him in the eye, which I found A-OK. Being five-eight, I liked a man with altitude.

The fireman was certainly lighting my fire.

"Holy crap?" Pancake man, also known as Mr. Strickland, replied.

Flustered, I tried to smile, but I was mortified. Not because I'd said holy crap. That had just slipped out. I could have probably come up with something better, but holy crap, he was the fireman who'd come into the store for the fire inspection. The one with the Whopper Dong. The one who—

"I know you," Ty said, smiling. Damn. His teeth were straight and perfect. I could feel my blood pressure going through the roof. No bacon for breakfast for me or I might have an embolism on the spot. "You're Jane from Goldilocks."

His smile widened into a full-on grin. Yeah, he remembered me and the array of dildos.

"You know Mom from work?" asked Bobby, eyeing both of us curiously. His plate was filled with food and he needed two hands to carry it. "Mom says her work is for grown-ups."

Ty nodded his head and looked Bobby in the eye. "I

had to inspect the sprinkler system and make sure there are fire extinguishers in the store. I was working, too."

"Boys, take your plates and find a place to sit." I angled my head toward the tables. "I'll be right there."

"Will you sit with us, Mr. Strickland?" Zach asked, full of hope.

"Why don't you two call me Ty, all right?"

The boys nodded their heads.

"Give me a few minutes to finish here and I'll join you," Ty replied, holding up his metal tongs to prove he had serious work to do. The kids scurried off to scarf down their meals. Ty watched the boys go then turned his gaze to me. Grinned some more.

"I learned a lot from you at the store yesterday," Ty said. He appeared to be enjoying himself immensely. Me, not so much. Mr. Tall, Light and Handsome was... was flirting with me.

Standing in the pancake line, I did a quick mental inventory. It wasn't quite eight in the morning so I wasn't at my best. On a good day, or at least later in the morning, I liked to think of myself as better than average looking. I'm above average in height, longer than average in curly, dark blond hair, larger than average in breast size, and lighter than average in weight. The weight part I could thank my mom. Like her, I can eat whatever I wanted and not gain an ounce.

My best friend Kelly hated me for that, but what could I do? She should hate my mother instead.

The downside to being skinny was that I had no calves. None. It was a straight shot down from knobby knees to feet. I could run until the cows came home and I wouldn't develop calves. At least Kelly had calves. The rest, including the calves, was just weird genetics.

Of course, this morning I hadn't pulled myself together as I should, or how Kelly said I should. I was what was called a low maintenance woman. I didn't even think I had a can of hairspray in my house.

I went over the crucial things in my mind. Hair, breath, bra, zipper. At least I'd brushed my teeth, but my hair was pulled up into a ratty ponytail, probably curls sticking out every which way. I wore shorts—the zipper was up, an old Sweet Pea Festival T-shirt and flip-flops. No make-up. It couldn't have gotten much worse unless I had decided to skip a bra. Which, being a 34D, would have been *really* bad.

I was a mess! Kelly would disavow any knowledge of me if she came through the door.

Then I remembered Ty was my new neighbor. No matter how much I felt like it at the moment, I couldn't hide from him forever.

What could this guy see in me besides a complete slob who was an expert in dildos? What had I worn yesterday? It didn't matter. He'd probably been too blinded by all the sex toys to have noticed my clothing. I felt like a total freak. And yet he was flirting.

"This is one of those embarrassing moments in life." I pointed my finger at him. Hot or not, I felt very cranky. How dare he flirt with me when I was unprepared! "You need to tell me a secret about you so it balances out."

A corner of his mouth tipped up into a grin. "Fair enough." He leaned toward me over the platter of pancakes, looked to the left and right and whispered so only I could hear. "I can see the perks of the silicone dildo you talked about yesterday, even the one with the top that rotates." He twirled his finger in the air to demonstrate, then looked me straight in the eye. "But I like a woman who goes for the real thing."

Was that steam coming up off the platter of pancakes I was leaning over, or did I just break out in sweat?

Read more Montana Fire now!

ABOUT THE AUTHOR

Vanessa Vale is the *USA Today* Bestselling author of over 40 books, sexy romance novels, including her popular Bridgewater historical romance series and hot contemporary romances featuring unapologetic bad boys who don't just fall in love, they fall hard. When she's not writing, Vanessa savors the insanity of raising two boys, is figuring out how many meals she can make with a pressure cooker, and teaches a pretty mean karate class. While she's not as skilled at social media as her kids, she loves to interact with readers.

Instagram

www.vanessavaleauthor.com

ALSO BY VANESSA VALE

Steele Ranch

Spurred

Wrangled

Tangled

Hitched

Lassoed

Bridgewater County Series

Ride Me Dirty

Claim Me Hard

Take Me Fast

Hold Me Close

Make Me Yours

Kiss Me Crazy

Mail Order Bride of Slate Springs Series

A Wanton Woman

A Wild Woman

A Wicked Woman

Bridgewater Ménage Series

Their Runaway Bride

Standalone Reads